CW00505451

Chris Fogg is a creative producer, writer, director and dramaturg, who has written and directed for the theatre for many years, as well as collaborating artistically with choreographers and contemporary dance companies.

He has written more than thirty works for the stage as well as four collections of poems, stories and essays. These are: *Special Relationships, Northern Songs, Painting by Numbers* and *Dawn Chorus* (with woodcut illustrations by Chris Waters), all published by Mudlark Press.

Several of Chris's poems have appeared in International Psychoanalysis (IP), a US online journal, as well as in *Climate of Opinion*, a selection of verse in response to the work of Sigmund Freud edited by Irene Willis, and *What They Bring: The Poetry of Migration & Immigration*, co-edited by Irene Willis and Jim Haba, each published by IP in 2017 and 2020.

In 2022 Chris completed *Ornaments of Grace*, a sequence of 12 novels all set in Manchester, described as 'a love letter to the city', published by Flax Books.

Theatre works by Chris Fogg

The Tall Tree*
To See the Six Points* (*with music by Chris Dumigan*)
The Silent Princess
Changeling
Peterloo: The Greatest Show on Earth
Snapshot (*co-written with Andrew Pastor & Chris Phillips*)
Safe Haven
Firestarter
Trying to Get Back Home
Heroes
Bogus
It's Not Just The Jewels...
You Are Harry Kipper & I Claim My Five Pounds!
One of Us**
How To Build A Rocket** (*writing assistant to Gavin Stride*)
All The Ghosts Walk With Us (*with Laila Diallo & Phil King*)
Posting to Iraq
Tree House
The Time of Our Lives (*for Wassail Theatre*)

Adaptations:
1984
Follow the Malachite (*adapted from The Stone Book Quartet*)
Return of the Native
The Birdman (*adapted from the Melvyn Burgess children's book*)

For young people and community companies:
The Ballad of Billy the Kid
Market Forces
Small Blue Thing
Inside
The Sleeping Clock
Titanic
The Posy Tree
Scheherazade
Persons Reported

Musicals: (*co-written with Chris Dumigan*)
Stag
Marilyn

2

Poems, Short Stories & Essays by Chris Fogg

Special Relationships
Northern Songs
Painting by Numbers
Dawn Chorus *(with woodcut illustrations by Chris Waters)*

Novels (Ornaments of Grace)

Pomona
Enclave
Nymphs & Shepherds
The Spindle Tree
Return
Kettle
Litmus
A Grain of Mustard Seed
The Waxing of a Great Tree
All the Fowls of the Air
The Principal Thing
A Crown of Glory

Back Stories

poems, short stories and essays

by

Chris Fogg

flaxbooks

First published 2023
© Chris Fogg 2023

Chris Fogg has asserted his rights under Copyright Designs & Patents Act 1988 to be identified as the author of this book

ISBN Number: 9798850994853

Cover Photos: Shirley Baker

Printed in Great Britain by Amazon

for Amanda & Tim

Foreword

"It's hard when folk can't find their work
Where they've been bred and born..."

All the poems, stories and essays presented here in *Back Stories* first appeared in one of three earlier collections – *Special Relationships, Northern Songs* or *Painting by Numbers* – since when they have been revisited, revised, re-imagined and re-ordered to tell the story of a boy growing up in a northern town in the 60s and 70s.

People say that if you can remember the 60s, then you can't really have been there. I disagree. There was far more to that wondrous decade than Swinging London, Beatlemania, sex, drugs and rock & roll (although each of those puts in an appearance here). But there was also the grime of living and working in the shadow of Irlam Steel Works close to the toxic sludge of the Manchester Ship Canal, and that the changes happening in society during those tumultuous times might offer the promise of escape and the hope of a different life.

Back Stories recall those formative years. Wordsworth tells us that the child is father to the man. These are the tales of my particular childhood and teenage years. But I hope they resonate with your own growing up, for such experiences are, I believe, universal and timeless, as well as personal and specific.

"From forges, mills and coaling boats
Good Lord, deliver me..." (The Dalesman's Litany: Traditional)

Special thanks to:
Brian Hesketh and Jennie Banks for invaluable technical assistance, and the poets Chris Waters and Irene Willis for their constant encouragement and support.

Contents

1

Family Album

Family Trees

this is a story my mother told me
it's about her great great granddad
who lived with his family on the Moss

every evening after work he'd go
to the family cow, lie on its back
his head between its horns

and teach himself to read, my mother
said her granddad told this story
often like reciting catechism

it was what inspired him he'd say...
now there's a plaque in the Wesleyan
chapel in his honour plus a street

named after him – Albert Street –
(my mum's granddad, not the Prince Consort)
behind the printing works my granddad's
mother set up when she was a widow

(before that she'd been a lacemaker) -
all are there still, testimonials
to their endurance (except the cow

and the book) what book was it I wonder
framed by the huge sky of Cadishead Moss
that so made him want to read?

                              *

my uncle Stanley never learnt to read
never needed to, he said, he was what
we used to call a little simple
I remember him as a jolly man

with a red face and a high squeaky voice
a bit like Mr Punch he made me laugh

he used words like Jimmy Riddle and
he taught me how to play gin rummy

he never went to school, he'd slip off
to the fields and bring home injured rabbits
dead voles, live adders, which my gran (his
sister) had to get rid of before their dad

(a miner) brought his temper home from work
but mostly what my uncle Stanley
studied were birds - he had a way with them
he ringed them, nursed them, later bred them

finches, love-birds, canaries - he became
something of an expert in them, people
wrote to him from all over the world
to seek his advice, my auntie Ruby

(Stan's wife) would read the letters to him
he answered them all, he was the first
person to breed a white budgerigar
after that he let his birds go free

I remember him at family funerals
sitting in the kitchen with the women
he'd take me on his knee and produce
pennies from behind my ear

*

all families have their characters
their stories - these are just a few of mine

I tell them to our son, I pass them on
in the hope that he will in his turn

pass them on to his own children
my stories make him laugh for they're no more

real to him than the imaginary friends
he talks to when he's climbing trees

which he does in the garden, making complex
routes among the branches which he tries

to follow but something always distracts
him, he has to start again, he makes up

new rules every time whistling as he
swings casually from the highest branch

the past does not concern him -
I too follow complicated routes

of my own making, I think I know
the way I want to go but always

something checks me nudging me towards
a path I meant to shun - a pair of horns

prodding me in the back, a white
bird flying across the sun...

Sunday Afternoons...

…began straight after breakfast
when my grandmother would scrub
the back of my neck with a pumice stone

hair was brushed and brylcreemed
shoes polished to a mirror
and to cap it all
I had to wear a tie

… but worse than all of this
was having always to be quiet –
never speak unless spoken to
was an unbreakable rule

forced to sit still and listen
to the boring talk of adults
I wasn't allowed to read a book
or colour in, or even play Patience

my swinging legs suspended
by the merest of stern glances
the faintest fidget frozen
by a single raised finger

… I could imagine no worse fate
than to grow up
willingly choosing to endure
the strain of those Sunday silences

Aunts & Uncles, part 1: Enate

At the start of *'Annie Hall'* Woody Allen repeats the old Groucho Marx joke that he would never want to join a club which had him as a member. But your family is a club you are born into and, as the saying goes, you can choose your friends, but not your family.

My own family falls into that much-loved cliché of soccer commentators – a game of two halves – for while my mother was an only child, *her* mother, my grandmother, was one of ten children, and my grandfather one of five, so there were always different aunts, uncles and cousins to call on, Wrights and Eves, Heaths and Blundells, each with their own particular foibles, and I quickly got to know them all….

First there was Uncle Cyril, who sat me on his knee and pinched and squeezed me too hard, who gave me a David Nixon Conjuring Set for Christmas, from which I tried to do one of the tricks at Waldini's Talent Show in Happy Valley, Llandudno, but which, to my eternal mortification, I failed at miserably. Auntie Alice, Uncle Cyril's wife, who played the piano for Saturday sing-alongs at the Legion but only hymns on Sundays, both sung with same wheezy smoker's hack.

Then there was Uncle Harry, a foreman at the print works run by my grandfather, who lived in the house where my mum had been born, who rubbed my cheeks with the stubble on his chin, who called me a closet seat, a big girl's blouse, but who would melt like butter for Auntie May, his wife, who polished the chapel brasses.

Cousin Dorothy, their daughter, who caused a scandal by marrying a Catholic and moving to Cheshire, whose daughter Julie I had a crush on, whose best friend was another cousin, Janice, who cut my hair and rode horses on the farm at Barton Moss with her mum Marjorie, who'd once been a showgirl, a dancer in the music hall, but who now mucked out the stables.

Red-faced Uncle Jack, who tied my mum to a tree in the orchard in the neighbouring farm at Rixton, where pigs rooted for wind falls, where thirty wild cats ran about the yard ruled by a fierce tabby with three legs and one eye, where Jack kept a succession of rolling-eyed guard dogs, and where Uncle Hughie, his dad, died in his sleep after milking the cows.

Dorothy's big sister Margaret, who worked in the Soap Works with Auntie Ruby, who married Uncle Stan, who couldn't read and who bred budgies in their back yard. Margaret's husband Bill, who drove a steam engine from the Tar Pit to the Steel Works by the canal, whose oil-slick, polluted surface spontaneously combusted one hot afternoon at Bob's Lane Ferry.

Uncle Frank, who lived in a converted upturned boat on a beach in North Wales, where we played cricket with an oar for a bat, where I got stung by a jelly fish, and where Cousin Derek, RAF pilot and Don Juan, gave my mum the complete works of Byron.

Uncle Tom, who lost his leg on the Somme, who worked for Tootal's in Manchester and who gave me a tie each Christmas. Aunt Mathilda, "our Tilly", who was the first girl in the family to work in an office (instead of in service) and who changed her name to Laurie because it sounded posher.

Uncle Gordon who made me eat black bananas every time I saw him, who did magic tricks with match boxes, but who we always had to be quiet around because he was an invalid. I have photos of him sitting on the decks of cruise ships with a blanket on his knees.

Auntie Ethel, who sailed away to Canada, where she bleached her hair and married a jockey. Cousin Alan who grew tomatoes in Jersey, Cousin George who flicked my ear lobes, Cousin Bill who bit my bum and Auntie Barbara who cuffed their ears…

(to be continued…)

Great Aunt Lily's Tea Set

(Scheherazade of the Moss)

Great Aunt Lily's tea set
sits now at the foot of our stairs,
a family heirloom in a corner
cupboard, fragile blue and white

china, twelve cups, saucers,
each with matching plate,
sugar bowl, cream jug, for those days
you were descended on by whole families

for high tea in stiff starched straight-
back crinoline, Sunday collars and neck ties –
you can tell that once its use was regular
for some of the pieces let in light

when you hold them up, crazed over
with cracks like Great Aunt Lily's
face, or how I conjure it,
for I've never seen her picture,

only heard stories of her
from my mother, so that now she's
the stuff of legend, and I conflate
her with the tea set, past its prime but

still defiant, as I imagine her
gaze would be if her portrait
lay before me on my lap with the other
family albums, daring trips to the Swiss

lakes and mountains years before
package holidays, no cheap flight
then, only overnight sleepers,
wrestling with labelled suitcases,

railway timetables and souvenirs
of walking stick enamel badges,
apostle spoons, my grandfather's camera
(an early Box Brownie) recording for

posterity with place names he wrote
in meticulous handwriting where
they announce still in immaculate
copper-plate Interlaken, the Brenner Pass

where my grandmother slipped and broke her foot –
the walking stick put to frequent use
on future bracing Cunard cruises
to Madeira, Cape Verde, the Azores

for grandfather's damaged lungs each winter,
then back home, to work, a printer
on the edge of Cadishead Moss
where Great Aunt Lily rented a house

from him, her own money all gone, caught
in the net of some South Sea Bubble or
Wall Street Crash, or the fall of Weimar's
Republic, some such calamity, all of it

lost, even her husband whose
name my mother never knew – he was
simply known as "uncle" – whom Lily met
while in Canada (he was trying to cross

the Yukon on a mule) and somehow their
lives collided on the wide open prairies
of Saskatchewan, (we have a blanket
still from those fabled far-off days –

Canadian Pacific). As well there was
a painting hung above the fireplace
in Great Aunt Lily's meagre house
stuck out there alone on the Moss

like some ancient lone pioneer
in her cabin on the frontier,
her homestead, her own little house
on the prairie, rabbits hung on the door,

shot gun propped up in the corner
ready to fight off Indians or a grizzly bear –
it showed a train, an iron horse
roaring across the plains, plumes of white

smoke belching from its belly as it
tried to outrun marauding Iroquois
and Chippewa whose war-paint faces
framed with coloured braids and feathers

screamed for scalps and justice
while Great Aunt Lily, face like a squaw's,
stoked the embers of the parlour
fire flickering beneath far-off teepees...

How my mother longed for that picture
on the wall, she never did find out
what eventually happened to it
when Great Aunt Lily died, when the house

was sold and all her treasures parcelled out,
but as I would remind her later
she had it still for it would pour
out in the thousand and one stories

she'd tell of Sundays at Great Aunt Lily's
(Scheherazade of the Moss)
where each week the prized tea set
all the way from Canada was brought out –

how it crossed the Rockies, canoed down rivers,
survived the Lusitania
before fetching up here in this nowhere,
this patch of bogs and marshes

still forgotten a century later
(two non-descript brick bungalows
occupy the nettle-strewn hollows
where Great Aunt Lily's rented cottage sat)

where every month she read from Old Moore's
Almanack sucking on mintoes,
savouring each foretold disaster
with such relish and delight

that if ever my mother asked her
some question she couldn't answer
she'd croak, "Let's see what Old Moore's
got to say, shall we? Oh yes,

nothing good can ever come of it,"
throwing back her head with a shout
of pure undiminished pleasure,
and away would go the tea set

until the next time when my mother
would gaze with longing at the picture
of the Indians and the Iron Horse
and spirit herself away there...

Now Great Aunt Lily's tea set
is an heirloom, a treasure
far too fragile and precious
for use, handed down, each plate,

saucer, cup pale and delicate
as an egg, a long dead dodo's
egg that can never hatch again, but:
if I hold a cup against the light

and if I flick the rim of it
I hear in the final fading of that
resounding ring Lily's cracked voice
rasping down the years

further doomed predictions from Old Moore's,
and though she believed every word of it,
she'd rock back in her chair, relight
her pipe, call to Stella, my mother,

a wide-eyed child of eight, to pour
another cup and damn the consequences…
Maybe if we took the tea set out
from its cupboard on the stair's

bend and drank just once from it,
we might imbibe as well that spirit
of derring-do, adventure,
indomitable recklessness,

risk and riot and devil-may-care –
but every time I pass it on the stairs
in what now serves for daily exercise
its low rattle sounds like distant thunder…

Ripping Up The Past

I found my gran in gleeful mood
in the gleaming, steaming kitchen; the smell
of beetroots on the boil; home-preserved food
in sealed jars crammed shelves on every wall,
and there, in the centre of it all,
singing while the rhubarb stewed,
my gran was ripping photographs. A bagful
lay on the floor already. "Would
you watch," she asked, in mid-atonic phrase,
"where you put your feet? I'm sorting..."
Then over to the oven to pull out trays
of scones: "For tea," she warned then, noting
my expression, scraped together broken
crumbs to stuff my fists. "These
can go an' all," she said, "courting
snaps of me and Hubert, days
long gone..." Weddings, Whit-Walks,
cousins' christenings: wide-eyed,
appalled, I watched her toss away Works'
Outings, Cricket Teas, Church Fetes I'd
heard so much about... *Abide
With Me* welled up while cakes
were brushed and nutmeg coated
on to warm egg custards.
Flakes of pastry fell like snow and
settled on the fading sepia,
a film on film, like a gloved hand
across the eye.

           That noise of paper
tearing cut the kitchen, drowned
the other normal daily sound
of song and simmering. A shower
of memories like peelings piled beside her.

"Why?" I wailed. The singing stopped,
she gripped my shoulder hard. "I've

28

done with 'em," she said, then tapped
her temple. "All in here." She gave
me her old-fashioned stare. "Have
you learned nowt at school?" A blackbird hopped
up on the window-sill, a look of
cold compliance in its eyes. From gran's cupped
palm it pecked some seeds. "Is it tame?"
I whispered. "Don't be daft – why should it
be?" The window clouded up with steam,
her fingers fountained, the bird twisted
in reluctant flight, shook its ragged frame
and, like me, was gone, as if it never came.
Would it return tomorrow? Ever? Would it?

I held that moment then; I had it,
I thought, frozen, trapped, unchanging;
but the years trick me – did it happen,
or did I just imagine
it, filling in details to force open
a long-closed door? Do snapshots cage in
memory or unlock it?
                              Occasion-
-ally my gran's would falter, hearken
back to reminiscences, uncertain
of a fact or two. "When I was a girl,"
she'd say, "I sang a lot. I had boys
eating from my hand. They all
thought I had the loveliest voice.
At parties – such excitement, such noise –
I checked my music, made my choice…
Most of them dead now, a whole
generation gone - Gordon, Jim,
so many… What use are these?
She tossed another bundle in the bin,
her fingers lightly trembling on her thighs
the rhythm of a favourite chapel hymn,
she sang, her voice now quavery and thin…

Outside the door another blackbird flies,
alights as I remember, and takes wing.

"Out with the old, a new broom…"

She burned a thousand photographs that day
and still I wonder why I feel the loss
so keenly. Is it the act, or the sure way
she threw each memory so casually away
that makes me down the years still cross?
"Photographs are lies," she said. "They
freeze time when I'd rather let it pass…
and anyway, they take up too much room."

Reparation

Why is it that my grandfather, who so loved people, elected to exclude them from all the photographs he took?

Living and working in the shadow of factory chimneys, cooling towers and spoil tips, the thickly polluted canal which one sticky summer afternoon self-ignited and exploded at Bob's Ferry, every year on doctor's orders he'd take himself away on winter cruises or walking in the Swiss Alps, the clear sea or mountain air bringing welcome balm and reparation to war-damaged lungs.

On his return he'd bring souvenirs and stories, the ship's log he'd kept, noting the minutiae of ports and currents, wind direction and temperature, a ritual he repeated throughout the year, tapping the barometer in the hall first thing each morning, recording each month's rainfall, and then off to his home-made dark room to develop the photographs he'd taken, which he'd place into albums, meticulously annotated in immaculate copper plate, date, time, location. But never, if he could help it, any people.

There'd be the occasional exception – the ship's captain, the mountain guide, a distant goat herder.

I have some still today, but not many. Most were thrown out by my mother long ago. I can imagine her impatience with them, hear her child's voice asking that same question – why do you take such lonely pictures? – and then my grandmother's practised response: "Oh, you know Hubert and his views…"

I wonder if the answer isn't much simpler. Surrounded as he was the rest of the year by noise, the pounding furnaces of the steel works, the twenty-four hour rolling of the printing presses, the ceaseless choke of traffic along the Liverpool Road, I believe he fell into the solitude and silence of those empty seas and high mountains like a Lethean embrace.

He told me once, when he was a boy, Liverpool Road was little more than a country lane; children would play whip-and-top along it undisturbed. It was 1910 and the newly-crowned King George V was coming to Irlam specially to cut the ribbon to open the Steel Works. My grandfather stood at the roadside to watch him arrive. He found himself a good spot where there weren't many crowds. A few minutes later a black Daimler pulled up and out stepped the King to stretch his legs. No one but my grandfather appeared to spot him. He took a silver cigarette case from his overcoat and then tapped in turn each of his pockets in vain for a lighter. My grandfather, then only twelve years old, did not smoke, but he had a box of matches. He stepped forward, struck one and offered it to the King, who nodded and drew deeply on his now lit cigarette.

"Thank you, my boy. And what would you like to do when you grow up?"

"I'd like to drive a car like yours, sir."

The King laughed and shook my grandfather's hand. "Here's a shilling for you." Then he climbed back into his car, which drove on down the Liverpool Road to the site of the steel works.

Five years later, larger crowds lined either side of it as my grandfather, having taken another King's shilling, marched with all the rest of the Manchester Regiment to overcrowded trains and trenches, to Europe and to war, bringing back with him a pair of broken lungs and a yearning for high mountain passes and wide, empty seas — solace and reparation.

Glass Animals

each day on the long walk home from school
I'd beg my granddad to stop by the hardware store that sold
glass animals
translucent swans, lambs with splayed legs all set to gambol
thoroughbred fillies that jittered and frisked
plus various assorted doe-eyed dogs
next to hand made ash trays with stick-on mosaic tiles
painting by numbers sets, embroidery for beginners
and while he stepped inside
to browse the mysteries of nails and screws
hammers and planes in the recessed shadows behind the
counter
I'd be left to gaze in unrequited longing
at this coloured glass menagerie

back then they were ubiquitous
like Tretchikov's 'Green Lady' and just as exotic
gaily displayed on black Bakelite shelves
asymmetric noughts and crosses
with round plastic knobs attached to each end
red and green and yellow...
I'd save my pocket money to add
one more captive to my gran's collection
polished and gleaming
occupying pride of place
beside the mantel in the inglenook
next to the clock my granddad wound
with a long brass key each Sunday after Chapel
where I learned to tease time

now time is teasing me
mother, father, gran and granddad all gone
along with the Green Lady and the clock
but some of the glass animals still remain
pale survivors

now quite retro, quite collectible
they'll outlast me
I'm looking at them now
on top of the shelves where I keep history books
a red fish, eyes and lips like a film star
a preening pair of blue cockerels
an orange Bambi, legs too long for his slender body
about to take their first tentative steps
a faraway look in the eyes…

Painting by Numbers

Time was – everyone had them.
'You too can paint a masterpiece!'"
(Even me, it seemed, whose art teacher once suggested
shaking his head over my latest pencilled scrawl
"Hey laddie – why not use a poker next time?")
'With easy to follow fail safe instructions!'

My mum and grandma, already able painters,
embraced them with enthusiasm.
Soon living room walls were lined with
Constable's *Hay Wain*,
    Van Gogh's *Sunflowers*,
      Franz Hals' *Laughing Cavalier.*

And so inevitably –
one Christmas morning –
a tell tale oblong parcel awaited me
invitingly underneath the tree
in the corner by the inglenook.

I lifted the lid of its snug fitting box
slowly like a treasure chest
sifting through its contents
like a miser counting coins –
wares laid out precision perfect:

   15 miniature tubes of paint
   1 row of 6 brushes lined up like sentries
   1 not quite blank canvas stretched on
   1 wooden frame
   1 delicately etched outline

undiscovered map
each blank country denoted by a number
for each tube of paint
each virgin sable brush.

Awestruck, I quietly closed the box.

*

Two days later –
after aunts, uncles and cousins had all departed –
I returned to it
opened the lid once more
and looked more closely.

Rembrandt: self-portrait.
Somehow sub-divided into only fifteen colours.

Obediently I followed instructions
filling in each outlined compartment with the requisite colour
rendering the old master's face into minestrone soup
each unmixed fleck and grain pock-marking the surface.

Always eager to please, to do as I was told, I slavishly stuck to
the rules –
keep off the grass, stay on the path –
never thinking to soften or stir, moisten or smudge
each separate pigment, flake of skin cell
knowing its place, within its outline, behind its wall.

Sometimes, though, my hand would shake
and a stray colour would wander off course
like Marco Polo exploring uncharted seas
beyond the edge of the map
the confines of the known world.
But the dried packet soup still refused to blend
steadfastly stayed apart
each molecule separate, contained
resembling nothing at all.

"You're too close," my grandmother said.
"Take a step back.
                    View it from a distance.
                              See bigger picture..."
But when I did so

36

all I could think of
as I looked at the enclosed patchwork fields
of a myriad different colours
was the dead conformity of the taxidermist
each component dissected
                              stitched back together
                                             but essentially
dead –
still *death* rather than still *life*.

                              *

Then the language changed.

Hang loose.
No rules.
Do you own thing.
Anything goes.

Jack Bruce and Eric Clapton were singing *I Feel Free*
and everyone was turning on…
                              tuning in…
                                             dropping out…

I abandoned *Painting by Numbers*,
left the face blank
threw the box away
forgotten in the attic.

Years later –
after my mum died –
clearing out her things, I came across it
shoved in a corner, covered in cobwebs…

Now they're making a come-back,
becoming retro, vintage, trendy.
We regard them with affection –
a post-modern smile –
as once more borders harden
with everywhere talk of building walls

pulling up drawbridges –
this desire to know where one thing starts
and another ends –
perimeter of fences.

I shan't take it up again
I prefer my boundaries blurred
to wander in the border zones of no man's land
to remain unfinished:

work in progress
empty space to fill in
blank on the map
above us only sky...

Choose your own adventure.
Make your own ending –
messy palette with mix of colours.
Dust it down.
Start again.

*

Sit yourself down at the piano
Just about in the middle
Put all your fingers on the black notes
Anywhere you want to
Sing along – write a song
And understand that you can play...
(Graham Nash)

The Story of the Moon

sick green pumpkin –
gouged pock-hole eyes
cratered nose
gaping toothless grin –

stared down on me
with murderous malice
between rows of bombed-out houses
walking home from grandma

she's hunting me, I'd
whisper, hand clutched tight
in my father's, unlit street
held no place to hide

her searchlight beam
razor-sharp would pierce
slate-less roof, broken glass
the long night walk home

shut your eyes, don't look
my dad would say but
even squeezed tight shut
she'd needle a crack

I'd hear the rustle
of her crow-black skirt
pursuing me, her deep throat
laughter's cackle

First Time in the City

first time in the city
and I am six years old
sparks crack in the cables
overhead the air splits
opening up a worm hole
in space time memory

breaking through my father's
shadow striding out of
sight out of reach and I
am always catching up
the moment that he turns
away around the next

corner trolley buses
criss-cross Piccadilly
rusting iron tracks tear
the buckling cobbled streets
past the soot stained statue
of Queen Victoria

starlings roosting in her
black bird-droppinged granite
shoulders her lidless eyes
hunkered down weathering
the onset of winter
and she is not amused

not even by Christmas
lights winking on and off
a just lit cigarette
clamped between neon red
lips mannequin's smoky smile
caught in the street corner

dance of sparking cables
millisecond contact
electricity crack
strobes the sky with splintered
warnings of tomorrow
mocking mirage of hope

my father drops his last
match the oil slick puddled
prism in the gutter
extinguishes its pale
flame as it flares and falls
I'm trying to keep pace

but my six year old legs
are just not fast enough
they trip, they stumble, fall
knees cut shins scraped elbows
banged and bruised reflection
staring out from mirrored

patch of shoe shine wet mud
I find a worn penny
place it on the gleaming
track before the iron
wheels roll and flatten it
slow motion spinning high

in the turning winter
air breath frozen statues
I lunge grasping at light
coin flipping through fingers
my father's eyes look back
you are never alone
with a Strand, a Strand, Strand

echoes thundering as
rattling trolley buses

converge then separate
overhead cables creak
groaning hiss of showered sparks
a hand yanks at my sleeve

tugs me cuffing my ears
watch where you're going where
he's going I follow
lucky coin no heads no
tails rolling down a grid
I look up and he's gone

marching into the night
the shadows swallow him
now the trolley buses
too are gone their singing
wires silenced replaced
by new trams' gliding hum

sleek and aquamarine
stealthy snakes instead of
fire-spitting dragons
one passes by me now
standing by the cleaned Queen
Victoria's statue

the starlings wheel the sky
world turned on its axis
in the half-filled carriage
familiar face looks out
eyes flare in sparks of light
window mists and he's gone

Aunts & Uncles, part 2: Agnate

My father on the other hand, the youngest of seven children, held no truck with families and was always tight-lipped on the subject. A guilty, lapsed Catholic, these were two clubs he'd abandoned – the church and his family – and we never saw anything of either.

My dad's father, John Fogg, died when my dad was just a boy. I grew up under the illusion he'd been a sign writer, who'd immigrated to a Salford slum from Ireland and proceeded to make his way in the world. I liked this notion that my never-seen grandfather might have left me messages in the signs he'd written, hanging over shops and factories across the city but this, like so much else with my dad's family, proved false.

John was in fact *born* in Salford, as was his father and his father before that, all of them called John. He worked as a labourer in a lumber yard by the Bridgwater Canal near Patricroft, where the waters of the Bridgwater are carried by the world's first swing bridge aqueduct out across the Ship Canal, which links Liverpool to Manchester, making a wide loop around Eccles and Peel Green, where my dad was cremated, and where his mother would move when she remarried, a fact I only learned recently, for I never knew her.

Tiny and fierce (I'm told) she brought up all seven children single-handed in a narrow, brick-built terraced house in Urmston till, one by one, they all left her, save my dad, the youngest, who finished school early at 14 to start work and help out, nightly trudging the streets of Salford selling insurance, by day a steeplejack climbing factory chimneys on Trafford Park, till National Service took him away for two wasted years.

From various hints dropped by my mother, I think my father never forgave his brothers and sisters for the way they all left home to pursue their own lives, leaving him, still only a boy, to look after their ailing mother who, when he returned from the army, had begun to lose her sight as well.

This was why, I was told, I never saw my grandma as a child – she was fearful, she said, that I'd fall in the canal at the back of her house – but perhaps it was more my father felt betrayed by her remarrying after all he felt he'd sacrificed... Who knows? As far as I'm aware he rarely saw her after that, although she did attend his wedding – a double wedding at which, as well as my dad marrying my mum, his best friend Bob married his childhood sweetheart Gladys – for years later, when cleaning out my mum's flat after she died, I came across their wedding album and concluded, by a process of elimination and the evident likeness she bore to my father, that this tiny, indomitable woman staring out at the camera, must be the grandmother I never knew.

I only knew there were never any photographs of my father's family at home, and when, once, I asked him why, he only said, "Not all families are like your mother's," and he never mentioned any of them again.

Auntie Alice Rose, the eldest, who I never knew existed till I researched the Family Tree, Auntie Florence, named after her mother, but whom I never saw, likewise Uncle Henry and Auntie Joan, yet they all lived close by. I later learned that I had walked past Uncle Henry's house, in a long row called Shaw View by the Candle Factory, every week on my way to Sunday School.

Then there was Uncle Johnny, for some reason my godfather, though I only saw him twice. The first time was when he came to our house in the afternoon of my own wedding, the second a chance collision on the corner of the street where my dad had been born and from which all these aunts and uncles had departed, until now, when Johnny had returned to live there with his wife and daughter. I liked him, but I never saw him again.

And finally there was Uncle Jim, who, rumour had it, ran away to sea, made a drunken pass at my mother on her wedding day to my father, and got into fist fights at the British Legion...

But now I doubt the truth of any of this. In the absence of hard facts we make up stories to help us make sense of who we are, and now I wish I'd done more to track them down, these relatives, the missing aunts and uncles of my dad, who I still picture trudging those Salford streets, or climbing those factory chimneys as a young man, and I'm reminded of what Thoreau wrote:

"Most men lead quiet lives of desperation."

My dad's escape was through singing. Each night he'd come in from work at the asbestos factory and sing a snatch of Puccini to reclaim some part of who he was.

If Sunday afternoons meant visiting relations from my mother's wide extended family, Saturday nights meant sitting in draughty church halls, listening to my mum and dad singing in the Concert Party they'd formed with Bob and Gladys, the couple who'd shared their wedding day. Afterwards I'd go back to my grandparents' house where I would spend the night so that I could be up bright and early to get ready for those Sunday family excursions.

My dad never joined in these visits. It was as if he, like Woody Allen in *'Annie Hall'*, although warmly welcomed by my mother's family, couldn't bring himself to join any club which invited him to be a member.

At the end of each concert, he and my mother would sing that old Nelson Eddy/Jeannette Macdonald favourite *'Ah, Sweet Mystery of Life'*.

"Your father's a man of mystery and no mistake," my grandmother would say, and she didn't mean it as a compliment. "You never know where he is…"

I'm beginning to think I might.

Friday Nights...

... I'd creep downstairs drawn by laughter and music -
my parents back home from dancing
or the pictures, enjoying a drink with friends -
and I'd perch on a stair I knew didn't creak
to peep between the banisters
first towards the kitchen, the men sitting
round the table playing poker,
the overhead light a fug of cigarette smoke,
and then towards the women standing apart
drinking babychams, easing off stilettos,
dancing in the hallway on stockinged feet
to Del Shannon on the blue dansette...

I studied my father's poker face
recognising the slow blink of his eyes,
the barely perceptible cat-like smile
when he had a good hand, and after
he'd pooled all the pennies on the table
my mum would drape her arms around him
cajoling him for one last dance...

It was then he'd usually spot me, or someone would,
a chair would scrape back on the kitchen lino
and I'd be beckoned to join them,
my mum would put the kettle on
for a last mug of Maxwell House
and I'd be passed around like a puppy,
cheeks pinched, hair tousled,
remarks made I wouldn't understand
till fast asleep I'd be carried upstairs again
dreaming of when it would be my turn
to enter that magic circle, to join in
instead of merely watching from the stairs...

Putting Her Face On

1

at least once each day, sometimes twice,
my mum would say, hang on a sec
I've got to put my face

on – I'd wonder why she'd had to take
it off at all or if she'd lost it
somewhere down the sofa back

Lonnie Donegan singing on the dansette
putting on the agony, putting on the style
what you pay for's what you get

and I would perch beside her while
she'd juggle compact, lipstick
fix her mouth in rictus smile

and tilt her head for one last check
no gash of red might smear
her teeth, or scar her cheek

switching on the Bush transistor
to hum along to Radio 1
winking at me from the mirror

then back to her reflection
shaping silent prayers up close
like sacrament, communion

she'd scrutinise the oval glass
for tell-tale signs of dried crushed
beetle blood before she'd press

a paper tissue to her parched
mouth to leave a ghostly pale
codicil beneath her arched

eyebrow in permanent thrall
dabbing scent like holy water
martyred cochineal

sacrificed in camera shuttered
compact-clicked posterity
amid the daily din and clatter

this tiny sop to vanity
catechism creed to navigate
each tell tale trace on holy trinity

of wine glass, wafer bar and cigarette
this marble mask a sealing wax
to keep close secrets locked in tight

2

a Tibetan mantra she'd say
to the oak wood hall stand mirror
before setting off for work each day

while I would swing around her
legs impatiently or tug her sleeve
latch key not yet reaching front door

this daily ritual before we'd leave
the house in breathless flurry
I'd watch our frozen breath weave

intermingling statues, the ferry
rising from the rolling mist
creeping up the estuary

 penny clutched tightly in my fist
to drop into the boatman's tin
fog thickening as we crossed

the ship canal towards the steel town
sleet gathering in grey flecks
the creaking wires' ghostly tune

breaks the scum-skin silence of this River Styx –
don't look back, she'd warn
the early winter light plays tricks

conjures shapes from iron dawn
oil slick lip-stick grin detached
from oar-split surface crudely drawn

and as the other shore is reached
one last compact-opening flip
to check the mask's still firmly etched

3

put a brave face on it, best foot
forward, if the wind blows
your face will stick like that

always a maxim or phrase
for what each moment requires
it's black over Jack's mother's

but blue enough to mend a sailor's
breeches, red sky at night
shepherd's delight, rainbow colours

lining her dressing table complete
with hair grips, make-up, powder puff
and my grandma's green vanity set

passed down the generations
(my wife has it now saved for those
extra special occasions)

rituals change – I now unclose
the lid on all those coded litanies
secrets whispered to the glass

smeared betrayals, sacred mysteries
she hid away with old love letters, pressed
flowers, perfect practised artistries

each cupid bow a palimpsest
I'd later try to trace, to match
my own, imagining them kissed

lifting a forbidden latch
on some frescoed holy relic
the lipstick blood-let leech

4

the record changes – Lonnie's been replaced
by Cliff: put on your dancing shoes
in stockinged feet she starts to twist

lacquering her hair her eyes close
remembering the mighty roar and rumble
of her father's printing press

she danced to as a tiny girl
wearing her mother's outsized heels
like those she picks up now to twirl

round fingers as she feels
the ceaseless rhythm sway her hips
turning piston, belt and wheels

winking at me as she skips
downstairs to where my father waits
brylcreemed and shining as he scoops

her in her arms – are we ready, are we set?
like me, she mouths in Monroe whisper?
uh-huh-huh, he croons with Presley pout

are you dancing, he asks her?
are you asking, coyly and demure?
I'm asking – and I'm dancing – and he's kissed her

squirm and wriggling by the front door –
let's rip it up and riot –
their jitterbug and jive will clear the floor

she lays a hand upon his jacket
last mirror check reveals her lipstick's smear
leans in close to re-apply it

5

and that's exactly what she did
again one Monday morning
after she had simmered then exploded

seemingly without warning
from kitchen cupboard clatter
while upstairs undiscerning

I heard her lunge towards my father
knife in hand, banshee wail
then watched him catch her wrist, hit her

hard across the mouth, slam her to the wall
the knife's sharp point quivering in the floor
caught and glinting in the stair well

stained glass light falling through the door
this marbled pieta frieze
dust motes dancing in the chiaroscuroed air

carefully collecting keys
finger placed on lips he caught
my eye, picked up his case

gestures haloed in regret
face in shadow like a shroud
stepping over her and out

motionless until assured
he wasn't coming back I watched her
slowly counting one to ten until she'd

strength enough to stand and touch her
cheek where now the welt and bruise
erupting made her catch her

breath beneath repainted eyebrows
she tentatively dabbed and winced
novitiate in a state of grace

zealot, convert, shone convinced
applying ointments, lotions, myrrh
hypnotically as if entranced

silently I stood in wonder
throughout this act of expiation
ritual of shaking powder

miracle of transformation
skin now white as alabaster
precious drops of absolution

beads of crimson primped on plaster
face of saints, eyes upturned
head flung back in rapture

catching sight of me she beckoned
I her ever willing acolyte
placed the holy objects on the stand

carefully selecting with her right
hand lipsticks as she seeks the prize
holding each up to the light

red, she says, it has to be red, her eyes
a shining testimony
words she will repeat the day she dies…

Cliff gives way to Lonnie
Donegan again, putting on the style
she'll brush aside the agony

return to face the mirror with a smile
I'll just put my face on, she grins
mustn't make us late for school

Crossing the Water

Each morning to get to school I caught the steam train that still ran from Flixton to Irlam, crossing the Ship Canal via one of many iron bridges. The canal incorporates sections of the rivers Mersey and Irwell alternately, linked by newer waterways constructed to provide an unbroken link between Liverpool and Manchester. When it opened in 1897, at just under 40 miles in length, it was the longest continuous river navigation anywhere in the world, and it led to Manchester, despite being so far inland, becoming the 3rd largest port in England. But it also cut off Irlam from Flixton irrevocably. What were once adjoining villages now became entirely separate communities, with different occupations and different ambitions. Whereas Irlam was all heavy industry – steel, tar, chemicals – Flixton became suburban, aspirational, a dormitory town for workers in nearby Trafford Park or Manchester. Crossing the canal became a symbol of stepping up in the world, so if you crossed the water at all, it was preferable to do it from Irlam to Flixton and not look back.

And so it was something of an anomaly that saw me crossing the other way back over into Irlam, followed by the short walk along the thundering Liverpool Road to Cadishead, where I went to school. I was accompanied by my mother, who was a teacher at the same school, and who had grown up as a child there herself, so for us this was more like a homecoming, passing on our way the house where she was born, the printers where my grandfather still worked, the old Rialto Cinema (next to the canal, but there the similarity with Venice ended), the Wesleyan Chapel on the corner, the bomb site on the Bama, the library on the edge of the Moss, where families lived in makeshift shanty homes built on stilts, where fierce dogs and feral children roamed, and where there was a gypsy encampment.

It was on the Moss, my mum would tell me, that as a girl she went to the annual travelling fair that pitched there each Midsummer's Eve. She loved its tawdry glamour, the freak shows and hoopla stalls, the rifle ranges and dancing girls. "She wears red feathers and a hoochy-coochy skirt," she would sing as we walked to school. (This was when she wasn't telling me the story of *Treasure Island*, complete with different voices for all the characters. How I'd been thrilled and terrified by Blind Pew tap-tap-tapping his way towards *The Admiral Benbow Inn* to serve Billy Bones with the black spot). The Cadishead Moss Fair also had a boxing booth, where a bareknuckled champion challenged all-comers. "5 guineas for the man who can go three rounds with me!" My mother's cousin Jack, a red-faced farmer from the adjoining Rixton Moss, who'd once tied my mother as a girl to a tree in the orchard and then left her there all day, challenged him but was, as he quite cheerfully recounted to anyone who'd listen, "knocked into the middle of next week".

But while there was some currency to be had by having crossed the water, it also quite literally cut me off from all of the other kids, who looked on me as posh, not one of them, even though my family went back generations there. A more pressing currency was to be found in the squares of hard pink bubble gum, which we traded fiercely in the playground, for each wrapper contained two postcards depicting various flags of the world, and I was desperate to collect the whole set of eighty flags. Frequently you'd open the wrapper breathless with anticipation, only to discover that the flags were ones you already had, and so exchanges were bartered and traded. It soon became apparent which countries were worth more than others. Union Jacks were ten a penny, as were French Tricouleurs, or American Stars and Stripes. Much more difficult to find, and therefore much more collectible, were Iraq and Afghanistan, Syria and Saudi, but rarest and most sought after of all was Albania. It was not uncommon, therefore, to witness the sight of young boys and girls tearing across the playground like flocks of starlings swooping and converging, dividing and separating, finally reforming around clusters where trading was most active, with as many as ten Stars and Stripes changing hands for a single Saudi scimitar.

I personally disliked bubble gum and never mastered the highly admired art of forcing large, round pink bubbles to blow up and then burst across my lips, and so I hoarded dozens of the thin square slabs to use as additional currency. Gradually my collection grew until it reached 79. Only Albania remained to be found. Nobody had ever seen it – the only reason we knew about it at all was because a full list of all the flags was printed on the inside of the bubble gum wrappers; we began to suspect that it didn't actually exist, either as a flag or as a country. Who knew anything about it back then? I asked my mum on one of our walks along Liverpool Road, and all she could come up with was King Zog, who sounded more like a character from a fairy tale than an actual real person.

Then one day, when the train was late and my mum and I didn't arrive till nearly the morning playtime, I slipped into Pook's Sweet Shop on the corner of John Street where the school was situated, paid over my penny for the bubble gum, and there it was, tucked inside beneath the hammer and sickle of the USSR. Albania. A black double-headed eagle in triumphant flight on a red background beneath the outline of a gold star. Each card, as well as a flag, showed characters in traditional costumes and a famous landmark – Albania has a young shepherd boy wearing a green waistcoat over brown shirt and trousers and a strange, conical woollen hat, behind him a lake and a snow-capped mountain – while the reverse side of each card gave snippets of information about that particular country (capital: Tirana; monetary unit: lek; miles from London: 1200), plus phonetically spelled handy phrases, should you ever find yourself there. *Loom-too-me-ray, Mik!* (Farewell, friend!)

When playtime came I duly showed off my complete set, only to learn that the bubble had burst, and everyone was into trading something entirely different. My collection had become, overnight, worthless. I have the set still, on a shelf in the room where I write; it has outlasted several of the countries the cards depict which have, for various reasons, ceased to exist, while another of its legacies is that I still know every single capital city, from the hours spent poring over these bubble gum flags of the world. I've noticed, though, that such knowledge has questionable value and carries little currency – girls were far less impressed by my ability to tell them the capital of Tristan da Cunha (The Settlement of Edin-Burgh) or Pitcairn Island (Adamstown) than they were by other boys' more successful efforts at blowing large round bubbles with shiny pink gum…

Journeying home back across the water my mum would continue the latest episode of *Treasure Island*, where flags also featured strongly – Long John Silver and Israel Hands hoisting the Jolly Roger on the mast of the *Hispaniola*, Jim Hawkins and Captain Smollett raising the Red Ensign over the stockade on the island.

I loved the idea of treasure islands, imaginary places with strange tribes speaking unknown languages, just waiting to be discovered. I drew endless maps with detailed landmarks – Smugglers' Cove, Skull Mountain, Devil's Hollow – and designed exotic flags for them all. So when, together with Pete from next door, Michael and Charlie the twins from a few doors down, and Barbara from across the street with her pet Sealyham terrier Candy, we decided to form The Cross Swords Club, it was only natural that I would design our flag – lifted almost in its entirety from the crossed swords on the flag of Saudi Arabia, but replacing its elegant Arabic script with the initials CSC. Very much in thrall to Enid Blyton, we referred to ourselves as The Super Six, and we met in our garage. Although we didn't have a car (and wouldn't until I was 13) we had a garage, where there was a coal bunker and a magnificent mangle with lethal rollers, plus an enormous metal wash tub, which were dragged into the yard every wash day. Barbara, who was very bossy, drew up lists of rules we had to abide by, and there were complex knocks and codes and passwords with which we would let one another in to hold secret meetings and plan our next daring adventure.

I remember my grandmother, quite baffled, asking me one day. "But what do you actually do?"

Wasn't it obvious? I rolled my eyes theatrically. We solved mysteries of course. We would lay trails – chalked arrows along the pavements – hide behind lamp posts as we followed unsuspecting passers-by and concoct all manner of fantastical plots to explain the most trivial of happenings: washing hanging on a line would be a message we had to decipher; sweet wrappers dropped as litter on the street would contain clues to the whereabouts of stolen jewels.

I also discovered through the Cross Swords Club the difference between boys and girls, as Barbara and I would pee quite companionably next to one another in the tangle of wild weeds at the bottom of our garden, taking care to avoid the nettles. (It was around this time too that my father, embarrassingly trying to explain to me the facts of life, got me so confused that I felt certain that, by handing Barbara a dock leaf to wipe herself dry, I must have got her pregnant).

Having a girl friend of course gained you more currency than anything else – even though you never actually went out anywhere, or even spent any time at all together. It was the unaltered ritual of it all that counted.

"Will you go out with me?"

"Alright."

Then off you would whoop like a cowboy riding your imaginary horse to join the other boys at the far end of the playground, running up and down the sliding piles of coke before Mr Nuttall the caretaker could catch you, while the girls hung about by the school wall playing complicated games catching balls and spinning while chanting unfathomable rhymes. My own special sweetheart was Margaret Ness, whose dad had emphysema and no longer worked in the steel mill, but was a park keeper, and who in 1961 put a shilling each way on the rank outsider Psidium to win the Derby because it was named after a flower. In a huge upset – so big that you can watch it still on Pathé News clips on YouTube – it won, coming in at 66/1, which meant that Mr Ness won more than four guineas. The next day Margaret, who had dimples in her cheeks when she smiled, came to school with a new ribbon in her hair, white for a psidium.

St Mary's School was surrounded on three sides by the Steel Works with Liverpool Road less than twenty yards away down John Street, a narrow cobbled alley between Pook's Sweet Shop and Martin's Bank, beneath a tall, blackened stone bridge, which carried trains from the steel furnaces to the Tar, Soap and Margarine Works further down the track. There would always be plumes of smoke from the trains and factories hanging like a pall over the school playground, and some days this would turn a sickly sulphurous yellow, and then there was a chance we might all be sent home early. (Unfortunately this did not happen as often as we wished). All the kids except me lived within walking distance, either from the Bama close by, or the Moss, from where many would turn up barefoot, or in shoes they'd long outgrown, so that their toes poked through the ends, wrapped up in newspaper in winter.

One day, shortly after Psidium won the Derby, we had a school outing to visit the Steel Works. I must still have been just eight, almost nine, but I remember it as if it were yesterday. We walked in pairs, crocodile-fashion, along the Liverpool Road, holding hands. Or, if you were put next to a girl, you each pulled the sleeve of your jumper down over your hand, so that you didn't have to make any physical contact. To my great delight I was paired with Margaret Ness, and she permitted me to hold her actual hand with my own all the way till we reached the gates where we waited to be met by the foreman who was to show us around. But it was not the thrill of holding Margaret Ness's hand alone which made this day so memorable, but what followed.

After standing around for a few minutes in awe, dwarfed by the huge cooling towers, we were ushered across the main yard and into one of the cavernous rolling mills. Inside the scene was almost biblical. I was reminded of Daniel and the fiery furnace; Meshach, Shadrach and Abednego. Years later, as a student reading Dante's Inferno, I recognised immediately that this was what I had witnessed that day. Great plumes of fire fountained into the air above us; white-hot molten lava poured beside us from enormous vats into cascading open pipes which transported it to giant bare-chested blacksmiths in the cathedral-sized dome of the forge. Their faces and arms bathed in an eerie red glow, they lifted these ingots of white liquefied steel with large tongs from the rivers of fire flowing endlessly past them and dipped them into dark troughs of water where they hissed, cooled and solidified.

We were allowed to wander through this scene from Milton's Hell more or less unsupervised, with many of those from the Moss still barefoot. After a while I closed my eyes and pictured all those Flags of the World from my bubble gum collection and tried to imagine myself in some of those countries, as far away from Irlam Steel Works as possible.

When we got back to school afterwards, many of the children were incredibly excited. Some had seen their fathers there, while everyone knew that their futures, in some respect or other, would be played out there, as steel workers or steel workers' wives. I was determined that that would not be my fate. I had found the whole experience a nightmare and knew that the only route out of such a fate lay in education. If I could pass my 11+, that would mean another trip across the water, to Urmston (the suburb adjoining Flixton) and the Grammar School. I was determined there and then to do everything I could to ensure that this might happen.

"There's no way I'm ever setting foot back in there," I announced to the teacher in class afterwards.

As you might imagine, this did nothing to endear me to my classmates. Later that day, during playtime, I got into a scrap with one of them, George Hodson, one of the barefoot boys from the Moss. "You think you're somebody, don't you?" he said. "You think just because your mum's a teacher, and you live in a posh house, and you talk proper, you're better than us. But you're not. You're just stuck up, that's all."

And with that he launched into me, pushing me into the coke pile, where we wrestled and fought till Mr Nuttall came running across and we both scarpered. In the afternoon, when were lining up for home time, Margaret Ness brought us both together, telling us not to be such silly boys and made us shake hands.

George and I became quite good friends afterwards, and we would work next to each other in the small school garden once a week, a blighted patch of scrubby land that Mr Nuttall somehow coaxed to produce a few potatoes each year, as well as some scraggy dahlias for the Headmaster's classroom, (Mr Coleman, who taught the top juniors, where George, Margaret and I had now reached, and prepared us for the 11+ exam. It was a small room, facing the Bama. Unlike the rest of the school it didn't have the benefit of the huge, cast-iron, pot-bellied stoves, which looked like monsters from a fairy tale and which heated the school hall, which was partitioned by sliding blue doors to form two classrooms. (Once, some years before, Margaret Ness's best friend, Penny Williams, who lived behind Prospect Library at the edge of the Moss, pulled my hair because I'd beaten her in a test, and our chairs fell backwards as we crashed headlong through those blue partition doors. Here I learned another of life's important lessons. Even though it was she who'd pulled my hair, because I was a boy, I was caned by Mr Coleman, while Penny was simply given a telling-off). But Mr Coleman's room did have an open fire, which George would come in early to light. He was still only ten years old and was always getting into mischief. Frequently he would shin up a drainpipe and climb to the top of the school roof, where he would sit astride the weather cock. Yet he was immensely practical and could turn his hand to almost anything (except for holding a pen) and so it seemed perfectly normal to us that he would be entrusted with this daily task of lighting the headmaster's fire each morning.

But for most, preparing for the 11+ was not really a priority. Their lives were mapped out for them. When the results were announced, I was the only boy to pass, while from the girls, only Margaret and Penny secured a place at the Grammar School. Though we would still be going our separate ways, for the boys' and girls' schools were on opposite sides of the town

I went to North Wales as usual to spend the whole summer with my grandparents, and it was while I was there I stumbled across an article in the newspaper they had delivered each day.

"Boy, 11, Dies in Swimming Pool Tragedy…"

George Hodson, the boy I'd fought with over our futures on the coke pile, the boy whose hand Margaret Ness had forced me to shake, the boy next to whom I stood each week raking the weeds in the school vegetable plot, was dead. He had just taught himself to swim (in a coal basin off the Ship Canal) and one day he had taken himself off on an adventure, a train ride across the water to the swimming baths in Urmston, and there he had got into difficulties in the deep end. But the pool was so crowded that nobody had noticed, and he simply sank to the bottom, where he had downed…

*

Two years later, I was still being troubled by dreams of George. You sort of knew that older people died, or pets (like Candy the Sealyham terrier who had died the same summer as George, leading to our disbanding of the Cross Swords Club, though in truth we had long since stopped meeting in our garage) but you didn't somehow think that someone your own age might die. This first intimation of mortality shook me completely. I had not seen anyone from St Mary's since. I was a Grammar Bug through and through. But one morning during a half-term week I woke up particularly heavy of heart after another dream about George gasping for air unheard at the bottom of the baths, and I decided I had to try and lay his ghost to rest.

I skipped breakfast and walked alone the mile and a half to Flixton Station to catch the early train. Over the iron bridge, I crossed the water back again to Irlam. As I walked down Liverpool Road, past my grandfather's printers, past the Rialto Cinema, the Wesleyan Chapel, Prospect Library, the bomb site at the Bama; past Pook's Sweet Shop and Martin's Bank, past St Mary's School and under the blackened granite railway bridge, towards the gates to the entrance of the Steel Works, I paused. I fancied I caught sight of my former classmates heading home from an all night shift (as in less than a couple of years they would) or pushing prams to the park. I turned down Fir Street, where Margaret Ness lived (though there was not a fir tree anywhere to be seen). I had not seen her since we had each left St Mary's and I didn't know what I was going to say to when I did. All I felt was that, if I spoke to her about George, she might understand.

As I reached her front door, I paused. A dog started barking across the street. From next door a woman with her hair in curlers underneath a head scarf, wearing a pinny and slippers, came round from the ginnel between the two houses. There was a cigarette hanging from her bottom lip. I started to move away. "Oi! What do *you* want?"

"Oh," I stammered. "I was looking for Margaret Ness."

"They moved," she said.

"Where to?"

"Mind your own business." Then walked back down

the ginnel.

There were a few kids now playing on the street with bikes and scooters – I'd forgotten it was half-term – and a couple of small girls were sitting on the kerb by the edge of the road unwrapping cards of pop stars from packs of bubble gum.

"Who do you like best?" said one of them. "The Dave Clark Five or The Swinging Blue Jeans? I've got these already."

"So have I," said the other. "I'm waiting for Herman and the Hermits. He lives in Flixton, you know. Our Gloria went across the canal to see him at the youth club."

"Was he any good?"

"He was rubbish, our Gloria said. Still, he gets to go all over, doesn't he? He's on *Top of the Pops* next week."

I walked slowly back towards the station and crossed over the water for the last time. I never saw Margaret, or Penny, or George, or any of them, again.

Apple Peel

Each morning, early,
before he set off for work,
my grandfather would eat an apple
picked and stored from his allotment.

He'd take the pen knife
from his waistcoat pocket
and try to peel it in one
continuous single piece.

If he was successful
(which he usually was)
he'd hang it from a cup hook
beside the kitchen dresser,

a looped, shed snake skin,
wafer thin, transparent
for my mother to see through
when she got up later for school.

If she found one was waiting for her
she felt the whole day would go well.
She'd hold it to the light,
marvel at the wonder of it.

She told me this story every time
she peeled an apple herself
but she was not as skilled as he was
and only rarely did she manage it.

When she did, her whole face
would light up with unalloyed joy
and you could still see the young girl
smiling behind the older woman's eyes,

even in her last week,
when she had grown so very tired,

and I was sorry I had not continued
this tradition with our own son.

Lately I've started eating apples
every day at lunch times,
removing the bitter peel which no longer
seems to agree with me,

and I find myself consciously trying
to do so in that same uninterrupted
cut my grandfather would fashion,
how he'd hold it up gossamer thin,

before heading out to his allotment
with me trailing behind him,
tying back beans, stringing shallots,
before the years banished me,

but as yet I haven't been successful
(not without taking most of the apple too
and that doesn't really count)
and I find myself asking:

who am I doing this for?

Water Features 1

Rhos Point '62
a wave somersaults above
my grandfather's car

lifts us in the air
drops us several yards ahead –
that was fun, he says...

2

School Report

The Bama

the Bama
Alabama

the Victory
the Bomb Site

a home
for heroes

with roads named
after generals

Haig
Avenue

Kitchener
Close

Allenby
Drive

the Victory
the Bama

older than
time or wars

O Bama
buried beneath

the crush of hope
and houses

built since on
the Bama

Alabama
lollipoppa

eeny-meeny
macka-dacka

der-die
dum-a-racka

chick-a-lacka
O Bama

between the barracks
and the chapel

the slag-heap
and the pithead

the Soap and
Margarine Works

Steel Mill
and Tar Pit

the railway and
the canal

lom-pom-push
the Bama

O Bama
the Victory

the bonfires burn
on the Bomb Site

our stamping ground
hunting ground

for cowboys
and dreams

The Wild West
Outer Space

anywhere but
where it was

Pentecost and
Tabernacle

Back Street
Bethesda

Dante's Inferno
the Steel Works

the Bama
O Bama

we played there
fought there

went to school
and chapel there

accepting it
never questioning

where it
came from

where it
led to

The Creature From The Black Lagoon
It Came From Outer Space

and landed here
the Bama

a maze
a rat-run

of back-streets
brick alleys

cobbled squares
railway arches

then out into
a clearing

the Bomb Site
the bonfires

the Bama
O Bama

the heart of
the Victory Estate

*

you can see me there now if you look hard
(we all of us carry our past lives with us
like the locks and chains of Marley's Ghost)
tethering my imaginary horse
to the railings by the school yard

I tip my Wyatt Earp hat with my Colt 45
blow across its barrel, twirl it once, twice
before dropping it from my fingers
blindfold into my hip-slung holster
scraping off the Wanted posters 'Dead or Alive'

in case somebody might recognise
this stranger who's just blown into town
I scan the scene before moseying down
past the Sheriff's Office to the local saloon
to drink sarsaparillas; a coyote cries

I look up, it's Peter from across the street
or the Cisco Kid, as he prefers
and this is his signal and everyone clears
this town ain't big enough for the both of us
Wyatt against Cisco, me against Pete...

*

turn the page, spin the kaleidoscope
past the hopscotch, whip-and-top, skipping rope
the big ship sails down the alley, alley-o
the Cowboys and Indians come and they go

Bronco, Bonanza, Gun Smoke, Cheyenne
Wells Fargo, Rawhide, The Virginian
Tenderfoot, Laramie, Wagon Train
fording the rivers, crossing the plains

desperate to know just how it feels
for once, just for once, to be Jay Silverheels
Tonto the faithful, the trusted right hand
yes, Keemoo Sabbee – who *was* that masked man...?

mountain man, trapper, staking a claim
for ever the loner, the Man-with-No-Name
with a silver bullet, clad entirely in black -
I close my eyes and summon them back...

*

there I am again, with a ray gun
space helmet from a cardboard box
climbing slow-motion up the pile of coke
stacked in the yard, planting home-made flags
conquering the dark side of the moon

or again, though much later, as James Dean
hours and hours perfecting that quiff
the curl of the lip, the shrug, the what-if
the cocky conviction I'd carry it off
this scrawny, pale-faced northern teen

*

Saturday Morning Radio -
Uncle Mac's Request Show!

Torchy Torchy the Battery Boy
The Court of King Caractacus Was Just Passing By
Once Upon A Time There Was A Little White Bull
Inchworm Inchworm Measuring the Marigolds

I Saw a Mouse – Where? There on the Stair
Davy, Davy Crockett: King of the Wild Frontier
In Gilly Gilly Ossenfeffer Katzanellen Bogen by the Sea
Que Sera, Sera – Whatever Will Be, Will Be

(did anyone *ever* listen to this -
apart from me, I mean, that's obvious -
when there was American Rock 'n Roll to be had
that made you feel good and that made you feel bad

on Radio Luxembourg, listened to at night
under the covers with a torch for a light
tuning the pirate frequency
that came and then went, but that made you feel free?)

No-one at all at school was impressed
when I told them I'd had a special request:
"For Christopher Hubert who's 7 today
who high-apple-pie-in-the-sky hopes I'll play..."

Like a streak of lightnin' flashin' cross the sky
Like the swiftest arrow whizzing from a bow
Like a mighty cannonball he seems to fly
You'll hear about him everywhere you go

You can buy all these back on DVD now -
digitally re-mastered, they seem less somehow -
The Runaway Train Came Down The Track-
I wonder what happened to Uncle Mac...?

The time will come when everyone will know
The name of Champion the Wonder Horse...

*

74

I un-tether him from the railings by the school gate,
stroke his muzzle, give him some sugar -
it's time to let you go, boy, I whisper,
it's time to take our separate ways -
he nods his head, nuzzles me, neighs
before galloping off into the unimagined night...

*

the Bama
the Bomb Site

bulldozers
giant crabs

with iron jaws
and steel teeth

gouge the
guts and entrails

chew the coke
and concrete

spit the steel
and slag heaps

into huge
storm drains

staunching wounds
and gashes

stitching scars
and lacerations

leaving multi-coloured
legoland to

seize the future
heal the nation

air-brushing
history

but look closely
now and see

we're still there
shadows, ghosts

palimpsests
shimmering

Wyatt and Cisco
Pete and me

and all of us
the whole posse

the Bomb Site
the Victory

O Bama
Ground Zero

in the ashes
of the bonfires

beneath the ruins
far below

a horse
lies sleeping

flanks like bellows
heaving

expanding
contracting

expanding
contracting

expanding
contracting

Carousel

"And the seasons they go round and round
The painted ponies go up and down
We're captives on a carousel of time..." (Joni Mitchell)

autumn was conkers
first you collected them
the shiny chestnuts gathering
in drifts by the roadside

then the preparation
the soaking in vinegar
the placing in rows on baking trays
to be cooked and hardened in ovens

next came the tricky bit
the piercing with a skewer
where, if you weren't careful,
(or even if you were)

it could split
an early lesson in life's unfairness
and finally the threading
with knotted string or baler twine

then you were ready
to do battle in the playground
a contest where for once size
or age didn't matter

if your nerve held and your aim was true
if you could withstand the rapped knuckles and near misses
if you had patience to wait
till just the right moment

you'd be rewarded with the accolade
king for a day
before your conker would crack
give up the ghost

consigned to playground tarmac
trodden underfoot
till nothing was left
but mashed pulp

you'd simply go home
select the next contender
start again
re-enter the fray…

*

winter was always soccer
pumping up the bladder inside the ball
like repairing the inner tube of a bicycle tyre

spit on your fingers
rub along the surface
lower in water in an old washing up bowl

waiting to spot the tell-tale
bubble of air escaping
drying then patching the culprit

before stuffing it back in its outer case
lacing the leather
hard and heavy as brick

then coat after coat of dubbin
to soften last season's shed-abandoned boots
mud baked like concrete

finally
ball tucked under arm
boots laced and looped around neck

you crossed the forbidden main road
climbed the fence to prohibited park
savoured the delicious sound of goal

ball rolling down rope of net
imprint of lace on your forehead
after you headed it home…

*

spring was marbles
all through winter you hoarded them
first in small string bags
later, as your collection grew, in large round tins

from time to time in the long dark nights
you took them secretly like a miser
held them one by one to the light
the glass-eyes, the alleys, the dobbers

laid them out and sorted them
arranged by size and colour
saved for the contests to come
as soon as the clocks went forward

you'd practise for weeks
on the hall carpet or kitchen linoleum
follow the leader, target, donkey drops
perfecting the weight and line

then, when the long slow thaw began
you'd blow on your fingers to keep them warm
kneeling in gravel till tiny stones
embedded themselves in your shins

*

summer, when you were older, was cricket
rooting out bats from the back of the wardrobe

carefully sanding willow blades
liberally applying linseed oil

till they shone like golden syrup
sprinkling talcum on the handles

unrolling slowly the new grips snug and tight
(like you learned to do later with condoms)

glowing cherry red in your mind's eye
you take the ball from its box in the drawer

your fingers close round raised stitched seam
eyes shut perfecting each grip

off spin, cutter, in-swing
leg-break, googly, chinaman

(since last season you've made do with *owzat*
exquisite tiny metal rollers

annotating each imaginary innings
with neat HB pencil in crimson hardback scorebook

between sky blue lines on pale cream paper
gridded calligraphy of schoolboy dreams)

now you whiten pads and boots, screw in studs
bend and stretch rubber-spiked green gloves

air your box, pack and repack your bag
then set off on that long lonely walk

from changing room to nets
pavilion to middle

right arm over, one to come –
rain stops play...

Kidsongs

intery mintery cutery corn
apple seed and apple thorn
wire briar limber lock
three fat geese in a flock
one flew east and one flew west
and one flew over the cuckoo's nest

This is the story about the Picks
Mum and Dad and seven kids
Billy and Sheila, John and Doreen
David and Brian (the twins) and Kathleen
Mum was enormous with nicotined grin
Dad was dapper, downtrodden and thin
He kept an allotment as nervous as a mouse
And they all lived together in a tiny terraced house

the big ship sails down the ally-ally-o
the ally-ally-o, the ally-ally-o
the big ship sails down the ally-ally-o
on the last day of September

This is the story of Doreen Pick
Who had to get married double-quick
The wedding reception was held in the chippy
But her husband-to-be proved equally nippy
He ran away, never more to be seen
Saddled Doreen with a kid at 16

the king of Spain's daughter
said she'd marry me
and all for the sake of
my little nut tree

This is the story of Big John Pick
Strong as an ox and thick as a brick
He'd play with an orange for most of each day
Till the hated Miss Brown came and snatched it away

82

Gloating she flung it into the stove
Triumphant she taunted him till she drove
Him so wild he plunged his arm in
Right up to the elbow and scalded the skin
Big John Pick was beside himself
He hoisted Miss Brown to the top of a shelf
A terrible silence there then ensued
Till somebody roared, then as one devilish brood
We raced to the playground a-rocking and reeling
Leaving Miss Brown a-kicking and squealing

bat bat come under my hat
and I'll give you a slice of bacon
and when I bake I'll give you some cake
unless I'm much mistaken

This is the story of Billy Pick
Who ate his own shit and was violently sick
At the age of eleven he still acted four
He liked to push plasticine through knot-holes in the floor
Poor Billy Pick never learned to talk
He spluttered and slobbered as though chewing chalk
His National Health specs were wound round with plaster
He tripped over bootlaces – a walking disaster
Always the butt of our cruellest games
We teased him, tormented him, called him rude names
But one day Billy Pick counted to ten
We asked him to do it again and again
His face broke out in the broadest of beams
A sunflower-sandman-smiler of dreams
This broken, lolling puppet-like boy
Moon-faced, transfigured, to absolute joy
We carried him shoulder high round the school
King for a Day, the Feast of the Fool…
I'll always remember the dinner-time when
Billy Pick counted from one up to ten

if wishes were horses
beggars would ride
if turnips were watches
I'd wear one by my side

This is the story of Sheila Pick
On whom Life played the meanest trick
She was the exception that proves the rule
Clever and pretty, the family's jewel
A university place beckoned maybe
But she had to stay home and help Mum with each baby…

little Periwinkle
with her eyes a-twinkle
said – "I'm going to the ball tonight"
but nobody could wake her
hard as they might shake her
her eyes were shut so tight

Kathleen would never say boo to a goose
She clung to her mum and would never let loose
This is the story of young Kathleen -
Went the same way as her sister Doreen…
David and Brian (identical twins)
"They've put them both in loony bins" -
Because they refused to co-operate
Because they never would separate
"They've committed no crime except being born" -
Mrs Pick had nothing but scorn
For the social workers' authority
"All they want's to split up my family" -
But none of the kids got taken away
Just another slice of life in this kitchen-sink play
Dad kept growing his prize-winning flowers
While Mum lay awake in the early hours…

shoe the horse and shoe the mare
don't let the little colt go bare
one two three four five six seven
all good children go to heaven

*

Inner city or stuck in the sticks
Every school's got its family of Picks

Now my son's at a small church school
With its fair share of jokers, eccentrics and fools
He comes back occasionally asking odd
Questions about the nature of God
Is God a woman? White or black?
Is God in the zip of my anorak?
At first I don't answer, then after a while
I say: if God exists anywhere it's in Billy Pick's smile.

Prospect

(former local library in Cadishead)

at the junction of
Liverpool and Prospect Roads
the edge of the moss

stood the library
two bay windows flanking steps
in white Portland stone

blackened by dark years
of steel-works-belched dirty smoke
hung above the town

sulphurous yellow
staining the stone like droppings
from an extinct bird

fading in the mist
rolling always from the moss
where folk still clung fast

houses built on stilts
patrolled by cut-throat pirates
with wild unchained dogs

or old wizened crones
who flung unwary children
in black cooking pots

hanging their bleached bones
on gnarled and blasted hawthorns
as wordless warnings –

keep out you, go back –
the huddled warmth and blanket
of books lay waiting

light burning behind
those two grimy bowed windows
to welcome us home

free from harm lurking
in fevered imaginings
rescued from danger

but when we were asked
what kind of books we wanted
we'd in a heart beat

clamour at once for
wizards, fairies, leprechauns
pirates, witches, ghosts

mysteries to solve
that thrilling frisson of fear
we secretly craved

to brighten the blank
realities of a life
whose only prospect

was the eight hour shift
the fiery furnace steel mill
Dante's Inferno

books were my ticket
my map for hidden treasure
over the rainbow…

the library's closed now
steel works gone, school boarded up
the Portland stone cleaned

housing a lawyer's -
wills, probate, conveyances –
duller, safer worlds…

Water Features 2

Clapton *'88*
we wade thigh deep through run-off
from rain-sodden fields

our son announces
adventures are fine in books –
I carry him home…

Flash Floods

Flixton '63
coldest winter on record
ice inside windows

frozen pipes bursting
torrents of water cascade
through splintered front door

misery for months
so cold the fire just can't catch
permanent power

cuts, birds stiff on wires
my mother can't stop crying
my dad hardly speaks

I retreat upstairs
huddled under overcoats
waiting for the thaw

doll in a suitcase
fixed stare piercing the darkness
scratches at the lid

*

later that summer
marooned by sudden flash floods
Chassen Road Station

rescued by firemen
who carry us one by one
like Angel Clare's Tess

to dry land safety
of Salvation Army hut
biscuits and Bovril

I miss induction
at the local grammar school
turn up in autumn

confused a day late
sans cap, sans tie, sans blazer
catching the wrong bus

with exercise books
not backed in plain brown paper
plimsolls not whitened

satchel like a girl's
grey babyish short trousers
belted gabardine

head dunked in toilet
taking turns to hold me down
repeat flushings

no fireman rescue
this time no break in the clouds
just more of the same

the weather forecast
prophesies more long winters
a cold front coming

                           *

lie low, my dad says
keep mum – what would Tonto do
or the Lone Ranger?

yes kemo sabe
white man speak with forkèd tongue
where is that masked man

I'm easy pickings
too easy, soon they grow bored
seek out different prey

I'm asked to take part
(if you can't beat them join them)
follow the arrow

obscure codes in chalk
mirror-writing on smeared glass
invisible ink

arcane rules, secret signs
complex hand-shakes and high fives
initiations

I pass the fire test
hand held over naked flame
thumb-pricked mingled blood

fingers crossed I play
the role of double agent
si kemo sabe

to each new victim
I leave a silver bullet
hidden in their desk

and keep making trails
of dead leaves and bird-feathers
a silent shadow

sweeping footprints
no longer needing flash floods
to cover my tracks

*

fifty years later
the floods return carrying
the detritus spoil

of lost memories
washed up along the shoreline
the rains receding

91

head of a child's doll
ravens pecking at the eyes
stares out accusing

a severed hand thrusts
splayed fingers through mud pointing
back where it came from

vainly reaching out
a battered suitcase bobs by
spilling its contents

guilty reminders
an assortment of odd shoes
and abandoned dreams

Age of Discovery

When I was 12 years old, on the last day of term before breaking up for the long summer holidays, I volunteered to do an extra history project. Sad, isn't it? I didn't have to, and nobody was even asking for anyone to. I simply approached Mr Vaughan, my History teacher, and asked if I could. Somewhat nonplussed he agreed and then asked me what I might be interested in. This hadn't occurred to me. I think I expected to be told what it would be, as we were the rest of the time. There was an awkward pause, and I realised he was waiting for me to suggest something. On the wall behind him was an early map of the world with illustrations of sailing ships and Latin inscriptions proclaiming *Terra Incognita* and *Here Be Dragons.* That looked interesting, I thought, and since I'd be spending all of the summer holidays in North Wales with my grandparents, where I knew my granddad had lots of atlases, I randomly came up with: "Age of Discovery, sir."

"Excellent choice," he said. "Here's a new exercise book. See how much of it you can fill up." Quantity, as opposed to quality, always seemed to be the benchmark of my school days. "But don't spend all the summer cooped up indoors. *Mens sana in corpore sano,* what?" And he was off down the corridor making his own end-of-term getaway.

My first day in Penrhyn Bay turned out to be rainy, and so my grandmother, who did not want me under her feet all day, packed me off to the library in Llandudno. This was one of those wonderful 1920's municipal affairs, with a large dome, imposing stone steps flanked by lions, marble pillars and an oak-panelled reference room accessed by a spiral staircase – absolutely the proper place to be carrying out important, serious research, I told myself. Fortunately there was a very good History section and before long I was rolling the names of those early explorers around my unfamiliar tongue like a litany: Amerigo Vespucci, Vasco da Gama, Hernando de Soto, Nunez de Balboa. I imagined myself discovering the North-West Passage, charting the coast of America, canoeing down rivers, hacking my way through jungles with daring portages through Panama, warding off marauding Indians, boarding the ships of scurvy sea dogs and hoisting the Jolly Roger. Much more drama than history.

(Why let the truth get in the way of a good story, as a friend of mine often says still?)

But the more I read, the more drawn in I became to the blind faith of all those who had sailed aboard such tiny vessels who literally did not know where, or if, they might sight land again. Spending half the year as I did in those days by the sea, it was easy to imagine that the world was flat, like a dinner plate, and that if you sailed to the far horizon, you might simply drop off the edge. The facsimile of the early map of the world that hung on my History teacher's wall showed a round, flat earth being carried on the back of an elephant, which in turn was supported by a giant turtle. I was also very much taken by Christopher Columbus's notion that by sailing west, across the Atlantic, he would eventually arrive right around the other side of the world at the Spice Islands, not realising that the little matter of the continent of America lay in between.

That idea of travelling in a perpetual circle, eventually arriving back at exactly the same spot you started from, continues to intrigue me.

For the rest of that summer in Penrhyn Bay a hot sun shone and I spent all of my time playing cricket, so when the time came for me to go back home to Manchester in readiness for the start of the new school year, I hadn't even begun, let alone completed, my voluntary project on the Age of Discovery. Hastily the night before I copied various bits and pieces from my grandfather's encyclopaedia and handed it in to Mr Vaughan on the first day of term. Clearly he had forgotten all about it and did not look too thrilled at the prospect of having to read through something extra he hadn't bargained for.

Weeks passed and, when half term approached, I plucked up the courage to ask him if he had had chance yet to read through my project and what he thought about it. Once again it was quite apparent that he had not given it a moment's thought. "Ah yes, indeed, most interesting. Don't happen to have it to hand just now, but first thing after half term – promise."

When the Christmas holidays loomed and still it had

not materialised, I began to suspect that he had in all probability mislaid it, or worse, thrown it away, and I said so. "Lost at sea, is it, sir? Like Marco Polo?"

"Are you trying to be clever?"

"My project, sir. The Age of Discovery."

"Well see if you can discover where the school playing fields are and give me twenty laps."

Rendered speechless by such injustice, I found myself lapping the football pitch at the back of the school, dragging my feet through the thick crust of mud which covered it. Round and round I ran, going nowhere, my legs as slow and heavy as that turtle's must have been, supporting both the elephant and the world on his shoulders. Round and round, back to where I started from. I tried to imagine myself as Amerigo Vespucci once more, charting every cove and headland from the Hudson Bay to Tierra del Fuego, or Ferdinand Magellan circumnavigating the globe, but I couldn't. All I could think of was putting one foot in front of the other, trudging through the mud, as the icy rain stabbed my face like needles.

Ten years later I remember a student friend describing a journey he had just completed across America. He was delivering a car from New York to California, a cheap way of seeing the country. For one whole day he drove through a corn field in Kansas, as vast and limitless as an ocean with no other features except the sky and the corn. The corn really was as high as an elephant's eye, so he could see nothing but the straight empty road stretching for ever in front of him. "I thought that in the end I'd simply drive off over the edge. Or go crazy. Like the Ancient Mariner."

Round and round I continued to run, finding a rhythm, feet getting surer. I began to realise that I had lost count – had I done twenty laps or not? – but also that it didn't matter. Nobody was watching me. I could stop whenever I liked, but I didn't. I kept running, round and round, on and on. I didn't know where I was heading, but it would be somewhere, and I would know when I'd got there.

It was my own age of discovery.

Cross Country Running

Every Friday morning, whatever the weather, we were sent out cross-country running. We were given a route – a lap of the school playing fields, then out along Bradfield Road towards the Humphrey Park Estate, across Urmston Lane down into the meadows (always flooded) by the banks of the Mersey, then back across the main Stretford Road to the school playing fields – which we were meant to complete three times. The PE teacher – the sadistic Mr Rapson – issued his instructions then breezily sent us on our way, while he stayed behind in his office by the gymnasium for a cigarette and the chance to pose in front of the naked pin-ups he had on the inside of his locker door, which he didn't know we knew about, and which we once caught him preening himself in front of.

He particularly liked to do this after he had taken the slipper to all of our bare behinds on some jumped-up pretext or other. Once, when we were mere first years, he left us alone in the gym one time and naturally we started chatting and fooling around, till the noise levels grew quite high. We weren't organised enough then to have someone on look-out, so his sudden reappearance caught us unawares. To punish us all for the noise we'd been making, he ordered us to form a queue so that he could slipper us one by one. A very quiet, nervous boy – Michael Stone – clearly terrified, begged Rapson to spare him because he himself had not been talking. This was true; Michael wouldn't say 'boo' to a goose. Rapson curled his upper lip in what for him resembled a smile and quietly informed Michael that in that case he would receive six strokes of the slipper to everyone else's three. Unthinkable in these modern, health-and-safety conscious days we live in now, but nobody thought to complain about either his bullying, or the lack of supervision for our weekly cross country run, and away we all went.

Except that for me, Ian Cloudsdale and Pete Jackson, we had ourselves our own private little wheeze. Pete lived on Bradfield Road (less than a hundred yards away) and both his parents were out at work all day, so once we had lapped the playing field, while the rest of the class trundled out through the school gates, we ducked under a hedge by the adjoining allotments and scooted on down towards the gate at the back of Pete's house, where his mum would always hide the spare key. Then we would ensconce ourselves in their kitchen, brew ourselves a pot of tea and watch the rest of the class as they struggled past. Forty minutes or so later, when they passed by on their final lap, we'd slip out of the front door and join the pack somewhere in the middle, having first ensured that we had splashed a few bits of mud up and down the backs of our legs to make it look as though we had been running down by the Mersey meadows.

To finish the race 'somewhere in the middle' was important, as we successively made our way past Mr Rapson's baleful stare, avoiding the random clips round the ear he casually administered to those within easy reach. Too near the front might have risked us being selected for the cross country team (which would have meant spending Saturday mornings with Rapson in the back of a minibus) and too near the rear would have brought further bouts of sarcasm, derision and, probably, the slipper – so the anonymity of the middle was the safest place to strive for – a goal that suited our whole school's philosophy rather well. Its motto was "Manners Makyth Man", and it was always impressed upon us that it wasn't really polite to win or excel in any way. Not that we needed any encouraging – what was the point, we felt, in running round and round the same piece of ground, over and over, week after week, round and round and round...? Done that. Bought the T-shirt.

To be sure, on the annual Speech Nights, prizes were awarded, but as much for "progress" as for coming top, and so that way most of us usually received something – a book token, always – although Rapson eschewed the whole notion of progress and only doled out prizes to what Americans would term "jocks", who would swat aside the rest of us like bothersome flies with the same dismissive contempt.

Of much more interest was the anticipated length of the headmaster's annual address, which was always interminable, made only moderately manageable by the book I used to run on how long his speech would be.

We all placed sixpence on the time we thought it would last, and if no-one guessed correctly, I would clean up. He was called Mr. Babb, Mr W.H. Babb (we none of us ever knew what the initials stood for, so he was affectionately dubbed "Wilf", and he had the shortest neck I can ever remember, giving the impression that he had a coat-hanger in the shoulders of his jacket and that he had just been hung up by it).

Afterwards we'd serve parents cups of tea. I remember one of the dinner ladies saying to me, Ian and Pete, whose turn it was to do this one year, what good tea-makers we were. "Well," said Pete, "we get plenty of practice. Every Friday morning."

Criss Cross Quiz

(Criss Cross Quiz was a TV general knowledge game based on noughts and crosses. It was first aired on Granada in the 1950's, and in 1963 a children's version was launched, hosted by Danny Blanchflower, former captain of Tottenham Hotspur and Northern Ireland).

when Elvis starts to sing
in German *Wooden Heart*
I know at once but tongue-
tied on live TV blurt

Harry Belafonté
instead (it's so uncool)
and I know there's no way
I'll live this down nor feel

each time I see the sign
'Granada Studios'
I blew the chance to win
on Junior Criss Cross Quiz

Amo, amas, amat

In addition to Mr Rapson, my school had its fair share of bullies among its teachers, as well as one or two who were truly inspiring, but it's the bullies you tend to remember the most, isn't it? Like Mr Johnson, the Art teacher, a bluff Geordie with a rasping tongue. He didn't mince his words and what few he chose to utter were by and large scathing. Once, I recall, while we were struggling over a still life he'd set up for us to draw, he walked around the class throwing out withering caustic jibes and comments as he passed each one of us.

On reaching me, he dismissed my admittedly weak effort with barely a glance, adding, while I anxiously chewed the end of my pencil, "Hey, laddie – why not use a poker next time?"

I stopped drawing instantly and have never been able to take it up again, although I love to look at art: visiting galleries and exhibitions I count among my keenest pleasures.

When Tim, our son, was just three years old, he was sitting on my knee one evening and I was trying to draw a car for him. With disarming, artless candour, he remarked helpfully, "You're not very good at drawing, are you, Daddy?" He himself has proved to be an excellent artist, a talent clearly inherited from his mother, and is currently working on a graphic novel with his partner.

But he, too, suffered from early discouragement. Like all children he loved singing, and would often be heard unselfconsciously singing to himself, sometimes songs he had heard, but mostly songs he simply made up. But when he reached primary school, his first teacher informed him once that must be tone deaf, for his singing was dreadful and it would be better for everyone if he stopped. Which is what he did, of course, despite all of our encouragement to the contrary, and still, to this day, you will not hear him singing. How differently things might turn out if teachers weighed their words more carefully. Parallel lines…

*

At secondary school, there were two teachers the memory of whose sadistic bullying has for ever stayed with me. First there was Mr Martin, the music teacher. He was a round, plumpish man with a chin beard, who misleadingly made you think he was quite jolly. He made lots of jokes and he would dash off improvisations at his piano to underscore whatever mood he was in or whatever opinion he was delivering at the time. But he also had a darker side cloaked within that gnome-like demeanour. Once, during an interminable hour in which he had us drawing page after page of treble clefs on a particularly hot summer's afternoon, I was sitting by a window where, outside on the playing field, a cricket match was taking place. At that age – 13 years – cricket was my absolute passion, and so naturally I found my gaze being drawn to events on the cricket pitch away from the treble clefs more and more, until, inevitably, Mr Martin spotted me.

"And what is out there, boy," he asked in his lilting Welsh accent, "that can possibly be more interesting than the task in hand?"

"Cricket, sir."

"Oh cricket, is it? What the fascination is in watching adolescent boys rubbing a red leather ball up against their crotch has always eluded me."

"Yes, sir. I mean, no, sir."

"So why were you staring so avidly?"

"It's the House Final, sir. I was just curious as to who was winning."

"So you're a curious boy, are you? I should say so – a very curious boy indeed."

By now everyone else had stopped working, scenting blood.

"Curiosity killed the cat, and besides, I don't think it's curiosity at all. I prefer to call it nosey. Are you a nosey boy?"

"I'd like to think not, sir."

"You'd like to think not, sir, would you, sir? Well, boy, I have a cure for nosiness. Step up here."

Sensing everybody's eyes upon me, I walked slowly towards the front of the class.

"Face the blackboard." It was one of those blackboards on a roller that you could pull up and down with the aid of a metal strip which ran along the bottom edge.

"Do you see this?" Mr Martin went on, and he drew a small circle in chalk on the board just above my head. "This is what we do to nosey boys. Place your own curious little nose into that circle." I rose up on tiptoe and tried to do as he asked. "Now put your hands behind your back and make sure you keep that nose of yours inside the circle." He then proceeded, agonisingly slowly, to raise the board inch by inch while I tried in vain to keep my nose within the circle.

"You're not trying, boy. I think you need a little extra motivation…" Whereupon he suddenly, without warning, thrust the metal strip at the bottom of the board upwards at lightning speed, so that it nearly emasculated my nose as it sped on up and past. The rest of class giggled nervously at my discomfort. "I'm bored now," declared Mr Martin. "Into the cupboard with you," and he bustled me into his stock cupboard behind his desk, threw me inside then closed and locked the door behind me, where I lay on the floor in total darkness, surrounded by piles of musty, yellowing music note-paper. He often threatened us with locking us in there; he kept a tiger in there, he said, who liked little boys, especially first and second years, for afternoon tea, and though none of us believed him, this was the first time he had actually put any of us inside, and the thought that maybe, somewhere, in a far corner, a tiger was lying in wait did cross my mind as I waited for the lesson to end.

After what seemed an eternity, I heard the bell go to signal the end of the lesson, followed by the mass scraping of chairs as my classmates stood up to be dismissed and leave for the end of the day. Gradually I heard everyone leave and waited for Mr Martin to open up the stock room door and let me go. Except that he didn't. I waited and waited and waited… In a panic I started banging on the door asking, please, to be let out. Eventually, the door opened and there stood one of the cleaners, plainly put out.

"Goodness, you gave me a scare with all that banging. Mr Martin mentioned something about a boy being in the cupboard, but I didn't believe him – he's always saying such things – you made me jump out of my skin. Whatever did you do to get yourself locked in there, you silly boy?"

"Mr Martin locked me in, miss."

"Did he now? Well then, I expect you deserved it. Off you go."

Not a shred of sympathy. It was like – years later – when I was 19 years old, I was in Newcastle visiting my then girl friend, who was at university there. We had just spent the evening at a folk club and after seeing her back to her Hall of Residence, I was walking through the city centre towards a house where she had arranged for me to sleep on the floor of some friends she had. It was just after midnight and the streets were quietening down, when round the corner came a bunch of skinheads. At that stage in my life, I had very long hair and looked, no doubt, a bit of a hippy to them, and I could see at once that look in their eyes – not dissimilar to Mr Martin's – which said, "Let's have a bit of fun." Instantly they set upon me, knocked me to the ground, and began kicking me with their not inconsiderable "bovver boots", only to be interrupted by an elderly woman coming out of her front door to wonder what all the noise was about. To my great relief, the skinheads ran off down the street and the old lady walked towards me. Looking down at me, lying beaten in the gutter, she remarked, "Well let that be a lesson to you," after which she merely turned on her heels and walked back inside, leaving me all alone to lick my wounds.

All those years earlier, liberated from the Music Room Stock Cupboard, I legged it to the bus stop, only to arrive there just as my bus was pulling away. Our school on Bradfield Road was directly opposite St Paul's, a Roman Catholic secondary modern, and such was the rivalry between the two schools that start and finish times for the beginning and end of the respective school days were carefully orchestrated so that we wouldn't all be arriving or leaving at the same time. By missing my bus, I would, I now realised, have to walk the gauntlet of all the St Paul's crowd, who would be arriving at the bus stop within the next few minutes, which they assuredly did. I tried to keep apart, hanging back from them, and this seemed to be working, until just as the bus arrived, a group of lads and girls suddenly barged into me, knocking off my cap, pinching my satchel and emptying its contents out onto the pavement, so that by the time I had gathered everything back together, the bus pulled away, leaving me with no option but to walk home.

When I eventually got there, I was more than an hour later than usual, but this caused no comment, other than a "What kept you?" from my mum, busy fixing the tea, to which I merely replied, "I just got caught up watching the cricket and lost track of the time."

On another occasion, once again bored in a music lesson, I was caught by Mr Martin as I was rocking on the back legs of my chair. "Oh," he sneered, with a growing glint in his eye, "so you like to balance, do you? See me after school in the car park."

When I turned up, he led me by the ear to a large stone pedestal that looked a bit like a giant mushroom or a font, which had a manhole cover on the top leading down no doubt to some labyrinth of pipes and sewers. "Up you get," he said, and I slowly clambered on to the top, where I stood feeling very foolish and exposed. "Now," he said, his Welsh accent relishing the vowels, "you know the Statue of Eros in Piccadilly Circus, don't you?"

"I've never been to London, sir."

"Don't you be clever with me, boy! You've seen pictures, haven't you?"

"Yes, sir."

"Well then, off you go."

"Sir?"

"Adopt the same pose. Pretend to be firing a bow and arrow and stand on one leg."

By this time quite a crowd had gathered. The giant stone mushroom on which I was standing was situated right next to the bike sheds. About 500 boys attended Urmston Grammar School at that time and at least half of them travelled there each day by bike.

"This boy," proclaimed Mr Martin, "likes to balance. So now he's going to demonstrate his prowess to one and all. I give you: the Urmston Statue of Eros! Let's give him a round of applause, shall we?"

Everyone started clapping, mixed with cat-calls and whistles, while I attempted to stand on one leg and hold an imaginary bow and arrow.

"Right, boy, you stay here till I come back," and off he strode.

The next 15 minutes, as I stood there while more than 200 bicycles paraded around and past me, were among the longest I've ever known. Needless to say, Mr Martin did not return any time soon. Eventually, the school caretaker, taking pity on me, said, "I'd go home if I were you, son. I'll tell Mr Martin that I gave you permission. And next time," he added as I climbed back down, "don't get caught."

More disturbing than Mr Martin, however, who was mostly irrelev-ant to us back then, was Mr Rhoden, the French teacher – or "Rodin", as he sometimes asked us to refer to him as, for reasons that will become unpleasantly clear.

Most of the time Mr Rhoden was great: he was quiet, calm, well organised, an excellent, methodical teacher with an obvious love of both France and the French, and he made us all want to go there, and once there, speak the language fluently. He tapped into my own near-photographic memory, setting us lists of nouns to learn with all the masculine words on the left hand column and the feminine words on the right. As I tried to remember them, all I had to do was conjure up which side of the page I had first seen them written down, and they would float back into my memory, and, because I experience synaesthesia, I still picture all the 'le' words as navy blue, with all the 'la' words being a bright, vivid yellow.

But Mr Rhoden had a dark side, and he would reveal this suddenly, unexpectedly, as if at the flick of a switch. "*Maintenant, mes amis,*" he would say, and we would come to recognise this sudden shift into French as a warning sign, "*amis*" flashing up in neon red for danger. "*Alors,*" he would continue, "Marat is coming round to see you. *Je suis 'Rodin'* and I am bringing *mon compagnon*, Marat, to inspect your work."

Marat turned out to be a long, three-sided cane, with each of the triangular bevelled sides sharpened to a pointed edge. He would brandish this before him, rather like a sinister magician's wand, as he walked up and down, pausing by each desk to check our work. Whenever he saw an error, he would remark, "A-ha, Marat is most displeased," and he would ping the wand on the top of our heads, which would really hurt because of its sharpened edges. We all of us dreaded the appearance of Marat. "And when Marat is displeased, mes amis, we know what he must do next, don't we? He must bring out his friend Madame La Guillotine," and down would come Marat again onto one of our cowering, undeserving crowns.

Sometimes, Marat in hand, he would pause by some hapless individual (thankfully I never suffered this particular fate) and, having admonished him with Madame La Guillotine, he would then insert his hand inside the boy's shirt and proceed to squeeze his nipple hard.

Thankfully he was replaced after just a year by the kindly, effervescent Mr McKenna, an ebullient cockney, who acted out his lessons with outrageous mimes, and when our laughter grew too uproarious, he would put his finger to his lips and whisper, "*Doucement*," and proceed to walk in a comical fashion on tiptoe, which we would all copy, whispering back, "*Doucement, doucement*," in a hushed, northern unison.

And finally there was Mr Lever, the Latin teacher – or Jasper, as he was universally known. His actual name was Johnny, but everyone new him as Jasper, even other teachers, I suspect, for he was something of a legend. I don't know how old he was – at 12 every adult looks old – but he had been my mother's Latin teacher when she was at school, so that tells you something, and he wore glasses with lenses so thick that they magnified his eyes to such a huge extent that he resembled some kind of ancient, giant bullfrog. His reputation preceded him, and we all knew about Jasper and what to expect long before we actually had our first lesson with him, which was as second years.

He had a ferocious, terrifying temper and frequently cuffed boys around the ears for no apparent reason, roaring like a bull till his face would turn purple with rage. On one occ -asion we rendered him momentarily speechless because we couldn't come up with the one word in the English language that has four consecutive consonants in the middle of it. "Come on," he bellowed, "what's the matter with you? Don't they teach you anything these days at primary school?" When he finally realised that no answer would be forthcoming, he

106

yelled back at us with incredulity, "Pulchritude, you imbeciles!" (We were, you will recall, just 12 years old, but it's a fact that has stayed with me ever since, such was the force of his presence in the classroom)."I don't know," he lamented, "education today, it's nothing more than a three-ringed crackpot circus. Why, for two pins I'd walk out right now." At which point, Derek Marshall, the class clown, would always hold up two fingers, offering Jasper these imaginary two pins, until one afternoon, when he was noticed by Jasper, who normally saw very little that was in front of him, and who interpreted Derek's actions as an altogether different two-fingered gesture.

"Are you saucing me, lad?"

"Who? Me, sir?"

"Yes, you, sir."

"No, sir. Not I, sir?"

"You're doing it again. You're saucing me. How dare you? I'll give you something to sauce about in a minute," whereupon he launched into a sudden and terrifying assault.

We were well used to Jasper's bouts of violence, which occurred on at least a weekly basis, but none of was prepared for the ferocity of this particular attack. He proceeded to knock Derek right around the classroom, up and down the aisles between the desks, until he finally cornered him near the door, where he repeatedly rammed his head against the light switches. The suppressed laughter that had greeted Derek's initial remarks had now given way to a frightened silence; it was as if the term 'shock and awe' were especially coined for this one moment. Although we were quite accustomed to regular beatings by teachers, with a ruler, a slipper, the cane, or, more usually, the casual back of a hand, the scale of this attack was unprecedented.

This was in the days when in the classroom the teacher's word was law, was never challenged, and we would never have considered complaining about such treatment to our parents, but something must have happened after this occasion, for we never saw Jasper again. He had retired, we were told, (which was quite possibly true, for to our eyes he was at least a hundred years old), and he was replaced by the young, good looking and dynamic Mike Ryder, an ex-fighter-pilot, who was also a brilliant sportsman, and suddenly Latin was no longer a dead language taught by some old fossil, but cool and hip, and I ended up carrying on with it right through to 'A' level, where I developed a life-long love of Virgil, Ovid, Catullus and Pliny (both the younger and the elder!)

I remember Mr Ryder walking into his first lesson with us carrying under his arm a copy of *In His Own Write* by John Lennon. "Turn to page 46," he said, and there we read:

> '*Amo, amas, a minibus*
> *A marmyladie cat...*'

And suddenly Latin was fun. It was John Lennon. It was the new zeitgeist. It was where it was at, and the three-ringed crackpot circus had found itself a new ringmaster. We had moved away from "*magister discipulum vacuum verberat*" (the school master beats the lazy pupil) to Mr Ryder's RAF motto '*per ardua ad astra*' (through adversity to the stars).

3

Summer Holidays

Cricket Bats

there are three of them
propped against the garage wall
glowing in the dark

biding their time, these
ghosts of Bradman, Sobers, Hobbs
dog my footsteps still

when summer-time meant
Oval-time and Oval-Time
meant Hobbs, chinaman

and googly, left arm
over fast, leg and middle,
bodyline, records

tumbling like apples
driven through the covers, or
caught out in the deep

till rain stopped play, we
retired to the pavilion,
this shed, this treasure

house of memories,
old score-books, numbers chalked on
slate squares, racked in rows,

an over-sized, white
coat hanging on a bent nail,
six small stones nestling

in the side pocket,
I trace their shape through the cloth,
turn each in my hand...

one to come, over,
the sepia photographs,
newspaper cuttings

peeling on peg-boards
pasted on the garage walls,
a roll call of runs -

solemnly we burned
them, all the memorabilia,
watched the ashes fall

in a slow motion
petal shower of memories,
like poppies on snow…

when we weren't playing,
for thunder storms, or during
the tea interval

we'd sit and listen
to archived tape-recordings,
mini-John Arlotts,

made on my best friend's
1950's ferrograph,
and relive again

past glories, run-outs,
lbw's, hat-tricks,
off-breaks, stumpings, fours,

straight drives, reverse sweeps,
spectacular one-handed
catches at fine leg

till suddenly it
was no longer just a game –
D'Oliveira*, he

roused our consciences,
made us see the politics
of slip, or gulley

of doctored pitches,
wrong 'uns, no-balls, skin colour,
and who'd be third man...

we played one last test,
to the victor the ashes,
sealed in tupperware

from my gran's kitchen,
with cardboard fielders we'd made
placed round the boundary,

arcane rituals,
hymns to fallen warriors,
we unwrapped the ball

crisp and new, a gift
from my granddad saved till now,
red as a poppy

we watched its high arc,
our faces tilted skywards
like stained glass angels

there were three of us,
bold, barefoot, brown as berries,
gilded by the sun

hung in that moment,
fine silk spun by time's spider,
caught in its web,

which still I can't snap,
ghosts of Bradman, Sobers, Hobbs,
whose voices buzz like

flies drunk on cider,
polite, lazy applause in
late afternoon sun

there were three of them,
cricket bats, totems, heirlooms,
they glow in the dark,

will not let me rest,
hand-made, first-bought, passed-down, they
hover above me

three graces, the fates,
cherubim and seraphim,
dispassionately

raising their fingers,
administering justice like
Bradman, or Sobers,

Hobbs at The Oval,
driving through extra cover,
or a deft late cut,

like a lover's kiss,
a host of angels' voices,
it sounds round the world

and I must follow
if I am to raise my cap
to the waiting stands,

spring-clean the garage,
reclaim the cricket bats and
win back the ashes

(* Basil D'Oliveira: the first black cricketer to play for England)

The Boy in the Wardrobe

He'd been sent to his room by his grandmother. "You've disappointed your grandfather," she'd said. "You've let him down." *He* hadn't said this, *she* had. And she was right, and the boy knew it. But he hadn't gone to his bedroom. He knew that there he would just look out of the window. Like as not the girl from across the way would be sitting on her window-sill, looking out too, when she was supposed to be doing her homework. Julie. That was her name, though he had never spoken to her, just waved. His friend Michael said he'd seen her kissing his brother Terry in the bus shelter one day after school. He didn't know what he felt about that. He'd never kissed anyone yet, except for his family, and when anyone kissed on the TV he'd turn away, embarrassed. Like his grandmother. "Stop it," she'd call out to the television, "and get on with the story." So he knew that if he looked across now and caught her eye, he'd wave, and then blush, and he would forget about disappointing his grandfather. And he didn't want to forget. He wanted to think about what he had done. And so he had crept into his grandparents' room and stolen into the wardrobe, where it was completely dark, and he could be quite alone, without any distractions. And that was where he was now, crouched in a corner, beneath the overcoats hanging above him, the smell of mothballs somehow a comfort, as his cheeks burned red and hot with shame. He had lied.

After a few minutes he heard footsteps in the hallway. He recognised them at once as his grandfather's, who had a slower tread than his grandmother, who never went anywhere without bustling. He heard him go into his bedroom and call his name. Then – "Annie…? He's not here. Where do you think he's gone? You don't think he's run away, do you?"

"Here, let me," said his grandmother, brushing past my grandfather with a flick of her tea towel. "Typical. That boy, he'll be the death of me. Don't worry, Hubert. I know exactly where he'll be." And in an instant he could hear her approaching the wardrobe.

"Don't think I don't know where you are, my lad.

Come out this minute." And she flung open the door. He tried to make himself as small as possible, but it was no use. His grandmother had X ray eyes, which could pierce even her darkest fur coat, and as the light from the window edged towards him, he shot out like a grey-hound from a trap and dashed back to his bedroom. "He always hides in there," she said. "He thinks I don't know."

At once he could hear his grandfather sigh. "Haven't you punished him enough, Annie? Let *me* have a word with him." Mercifully she told him to leave the boy be, to go into the kitchen and help her with shelling the peas. They went, and he let out a long, slow breath. Facing his grandfather would have been much worse than his grandmother's quick temper. He would have simply sat there, held his hand, and asked him what was the matter. And his heart would have burst.

After a while, his grandmother opened the bedroom door, looked down on the boy, and said, "Come on, Christopher. Your tea's ready. It's egg and chips, with mushy peas, your favourite." She smiled, ruffled the top of his head, then added, "We'll say no more about it," and he followed her into the kitchen, where his grandfather sat waiting. He was peeling an apple.

"Oh," said Christopher, "aren't you having any tea?"

"He's got his meeting," his grandmother replied. "I expect he'll have something when he gets back."

"We'll see," he said, still peeling the apple. "We don't want any fuss, do we? There – look." He held up the apple-peel.

"You've done it," the boy cried, "in one single go!" His eyes were full of wonder.

Granddad came towards him. "Go feed it to that blackbird you're so fond of."

"His tea'll get cold."

"After his tea then."

"If he's good."

"Oh – he'll be good," and he dropped the peeling lightly onto the top of the dresser, and winked at him. "I'll be off then, Annie. I shan't be late."

"Mind you take your scarf. You don't want that cold on your chest again." And he was gone.

The clock in the kitchen ticked in the silence between them, as his grandmother took off her pinny and sat down opposite him.

"Now then," she said, as he chased the last pea around his plate, "are you going to tell me what all this has been about?"

"Sorry, Nanna," he said.

"Sorry won't fix things now, will it?"

"But I am – truly."

"I daresay. And I daresay your tummy's better too, seeing as how you've wolfed down your tea."

He looked down at his empty plate. "Yes, Nanna."

"Well don't think you're having any of that chocolate cake I baked this morning."

"No, Nanna."

The clock ticked on, while his grandmother wordlessly began to hum one of her favourite chapel hymns, her voice quavery and thin. The cat strolled into the kitchen from the garden and, instantly sizing up the situation, proceeded to wind himself around his grandmother's ankles.

"And I suppose *you* want feeding now too?"

The cat mewed obligingly, while his grandmother got up, put her pinny back on and fetched the tin of cat meat from the pantry shelf.

"I'll wash up then, shall I?" the boy asked.

"Don't think you can get round me that way, but all right – you can dry." And she tossed him the tea towel with the picture of the Welsh Lady on it, then carried on singing her hymn.

Afterwards, on a normal day, he would have gone out for a last game of cricket with Michael on the field. But today was not a normal day, and Michael was a part of the problem. Then he would have come in and perhaps played cards with his grandparents, or scrabble, before a mug of hot chocolate and then bed. Tonight his grandmother said, "Well, I think there's been enough excitement for one day, don't you? How about an early night?"

Christopher knew there was no arguing, and so off he went to clean his teeth and get ready for bed. A few minutes later his grandmother came into his room, drew the curtains, and looked down on him. "Say your prayers, then try to sleep, all right?"

"Yes, Nanna. I'm sorry."

"I know you are. Now think on what you've done, and tomorrow we'll start afresh, eh? Goodnight."

She closed the door and he tried to say his prayers, but it was difficult, for he always pictured God as looking rather like his grandfather, and he knew he didn't want to look into that face and see those kind, forgiving eyes, not tonight. He turned over and began to look back at the events of the day...

*

It had all started the night before, when he'd been round at Michael's. He and his brother Terry were telling jokes, privately to one another, and giggling. Christopher knew that the jokes would be dirty, about sex, and that he wouldn't understand them, and that that would only make the other two laugh even more. He wished Terry would go out and leave him alone with Michael. Mike was always great when it was just the two of them. They both shared the same passion for cricket and could talk about it, when they were not actually playing, agreeably for hours. But when Terry was around, Michael acted differently, tougher, meaner, like he was trying to impress. Everyone liked Terry. He was clever and funny, good at sport, polite to grown-ups, liked by girls. But he was two years older than Mike and Christopher, and next to him, he always felt a baby.

Suddenly Terry was by his side, with his head in an arm-lock. "When do you go back, squirt?"

"In about half an hour."

"Not tonight, squirt – back home, to your parents?"

Oh." Christopher didn't like to think about that. He came to stay with his grandparents every school holiday. This summer he had already been here for over six weeks, and he knew that soon it would be time to go back. It was like when you turned over an hour glass. At first there was so much sand it felt like it would never run out. Then, when it neared the bottom, it all seemed to rush out at once.

Oi, squirt!" said Terry, rubbing his fist along the top of his head. "I asked you a question."

"Tuesday."

Surprisingly Terry let him go. It was as if for a brief moment he didn't want Christopher to go either. "That's a pity. Mike'll be sorry."

Michael rolled his eyes.

"And so will I," added Terry, wrestling Christopher to the floor and pummelling him with a cushion. "Tell you what. Why don't we all go down to the beach early tomorrow morning. The tide will be out, and it should be great for a game of cricket."

Christopher looked at Terry in wonder. He had never asked him to go anywhere before, not even to tag along. "What's the matter – lost your tongue? Say yes before I change my mind."

"Yes," he gasped, and Terry let him go.

"Get lost then, and we'll see you tomorrow."

Christopher ran up the passage that linked Michael's house with his grandparents', whooping like a cowboy. When he got home, his grandmother said to him, laughing, "Well somebody's happy. Look at the state of you, your shirt tucked out, hair standing on end. Whatever have you been up to?"

"Nothing much."

"How boys get in such a mess doing 'nothing much' beats me. Now – get ready for your bath, it's chapel tomorrow…"

Inwardly Christopher froze. Oh no. He'd forgotten. It was Sunday tomorrow, and Sunday meant chapel. Always. With his grandfather. Early in the morning they'd catch the bus to Colwyn Bay, to the chapel where his grandfather was a lay preacher, then they'd walk all the way back, along the promenade, arriving back in time for a Sunday lunch of roast potatoes that his grandmother would have ready for them. It was the only thing expected of him while he stayed with them. The rest of the time he was free to play all day long. But on Sundays he went to chapel.

"You've gone quiet all of a sudden," said his grandmother. "You're not sickening for something, are you?"

Maybe it was that which put the idea into his head. "I

don't know. My tummy hurts."

"Come to think of it, you do look a bit hot. You're not getting a temperature, I hope. Here – take a spoonful of cod liver oil and you'll be as right as rain in the morning."

He dutifully swallowed the noxious mixture, then took himself off for his bath. Once in bed he shut his eyes tight and groaned. How could he have been so stupid to forget that tomorrow was Sunday? But how could he let Mike and Terry down when he'd promised? He could already hear Terry taunting him, "Ah, does baby have to go to church with Grandpops? Ah, diddums…" How would that make him look in Michael's eyes? But how could he in all conscience not go to chapel with his grandfather?

He continued to toss and turn, unable to make up his mind. Perhaps at this rate he really would be ill tomorrow. That would get him out of chapel, but it would also prevent him from going to the beach.

Slowly sleep came, and the next thing he knew was the sound of the kettle whistling in the kitchen, and his grandmother's voice asking him if he was awake yet, and not to forget that he still hadn't brushed his shoes. "Goodness me – look at the state of your bed, it's like a jumble sale."

He dredged himself up from the pit of sleep feeling more tired and worried than when he went to bed. A stone lay heavy in his stomach. He wasn't ill, he knew that, but nor was he any nearer to solving what he would do. He washed and dressed and went into the kitchen, where his grandmother had lined up his and his grandfather's Sunday shoes on a newspaper near the door. It seemed to take an age to clean them, polishing them until he could almost see his reflection in them, but at least the task had occupied his thoughts for a further fifteen minutes.

He washed his hands and sat at the table while his grandmother brought him his porridge and a boiled egg. He could see his grandfather in the hall, standing before the oval mirror, combing his hair with a brush in each hand. He put on his jacket, then joined the others in the kitchen, tapping the barometer in the doorway before sitting down.

"Hmm… It says it might rain. But looking at the sky we might be all right. With luck we'll be able to walk back by the sea as usual. What do you think?"

"I think you should take an umbrella," said Annie, "and then you should take the bus."

His grandfather winked towards him. "Christopher?"

But he found he could say nothing.

"What's the matter with you?" asked his grandmother. "Cat got your tongue? And you haven't touched your breakfast."

"What is it, Chris? Are you not feeling yourself this morning? Come on, eat up – that'll soon put you right."

"I'm not hungry, Granddad. Honest. I can't eat it."

"You'd better eat it," said his grandmother, pushing the porridge bowl back towards him. "There'll be nothing till lunch if you don't."

"I'm sorry, Nanna. I can't."

"Can't eat was made to eat and…"

"Now then, Annie, he does look a bit peaky. Perhaps you'd better stop at home this morning, if you're coming down with something."

"And what am I supposed to do with him under my feet all day?"

"I'll tell you what, Christopher – why don't you go into my study and look at my atlases? You'd like that, wouldn't you?"

"Yes, Granddad."

"And you wouldn't get in your Nanna's way, would you?"

"No, Granddad."

"That's settled then, eh Annie?"

"You spoil him, that's what."

"Better safe than sorry. You know how cold and draughty it gets in chapel."

Christopher nodded silently, looking up at his grandmother.

"All right then. But I still want to see you eating some breakfast, understand?"

"Yes, Nanna," and he proceeded to eat his porridge obediently.

"Good lad," said his Granddad. "Right. I'd best be off." He put on his grey Abercrombie overcoat and picked up his umbrella.

"Don't forget your hat, Hubert."

"Thank you, Esther Hannah," he said, using her Sunday name. "I won't be late. No point in walking back without Christopher. I'll get the bus straight home."

Annie waved him goodbye and, as soon as he had turned the corner, she was back in the kitchen, standing beside the boy.

"Now then, young man," she said. "What's all this about?"

He gulped. He could pull the wool over his Granddad's eyes, but never his Nanna's. Hers never missed a trick. "What do you mean?" he said.

"You know very well what I mean, Frank Fanackapan. Now get yourself off into Granddad's study and read those atlases. He'll want to know which maps you've been looking at when he gets home."

"Yes, Nanna." And off he went.

Granddad's study was his favourite room in the house. As well as the atlases, which had fascinated Christopher for as long as he could remember, it was full of all kinds of unusual and interesting things, all of which had a story. His grandfather had been a printer before he retired, and in a drawer in the bureau he kept a set of old wooden printing blocks. Christopher liked to trace the patterns of the letters carved into each block. Normally he would have loved to have been allowed to spend time in there on his own. But not this morning. His head was too full of the confused thoughts that were whizzing round his brain like racing cars on a grand prix circuit. He had managed to get out of going to chapel. His grandfather had not seemed to mind, had encouraged him in fact to rest, which made him feel worse, because, while he had not exactly told an outright lie, he'd certainly not been completely honest, had he? And what was to be gained from not going to chapel if he couldn't instead go out to the beach to play cricket with Michael and Terry?

Suddenly the telephone rang, making him jump out of his seat. In the study the telephone was one of those heavy, old fashioned hand-sets, all in black, while in the hall was a much more modern one – cream and slim-lined with a bleep instead of a ring. He heard his grandmother pick up that phone and then – he was never quite sure what prompted him to do this – he lifted up the old black receiver in the study and listened in.

"2587…"

"Hello, Annie. It's Florrie here. I've had a bit of an accident. I was tending to Gordon and I left the tap running in the basin upstairs and it's overflowed. It's made ever such a mess, and I could clean it up, but Gordon needs me to see to him…"

"Don't you worry yourself, love, I'll be round in a minute…"

Florrie was married to his grandfather's brother, Uncle Gordon, who was an invalid, and who you always had to be quiet around. Christopher was just replacing the receiver as his grandmother burst in.

"I've got to go to your Auntie Florrie's. I'll be about half an hour, I should think. Do you want to come with me? Or will you be all right here on your own for a bit?"

"Oh, I'll be fine here, Nanna. You go."

"Right then. Mind you don't touch anything electric."

"I won't…" And she was gone.

Not stopping to pause for breath even, Christopher watch-ed his grandmother disappear round the corner, then dashed to the back door, where he picked up his cricket bat and, without a further thought, ran down the passage-way towards Michael and Terry's house, just as they were coming out into the road.

"We thought you weren't coming," said Michael.

"I said I would."

"Hey, squirt – what's that you've got?"

Christopher proudly held his cricket bat towards Terry.

"What on earth's that?"

"My granddad made it. It's special."

And indeed it was. They had chosen the wood carefully together, then his grandfather had fashioned the bat – both blade and handle – out of a single piece. To Christopher it was wondrous, unique, special.

"Call that a cricket bat?" (Terry again). "It's just a plank of wood with a hole in the middle." He turned to

Michael and clipped him across the ear. "I told you we should have brought yours – at least that looks like a cricket bat."

Michael wheeled away from the blow and hissed at Christopher, "God, you're so embarrassing."

"Oh well, we'll have to make the best of it, I suppose," said Terry, but then his attention was suddenly drawn towards two girls walking towards them along the promenade from the opposite direction. "Hello, ladies. Looks like your lucky day."

The girls giggled and tottered on towards them. "Don't fancy yours," whispered Michael to Terry.

"That's more like it, Mickey, my boy," laughed Terry. "Well girls, isn't this nice? The two of you, and the two of us. Going anywhere special?"

"Might be," said the taller of the two girls. "What's it to you?"

"Well we just happen to know somewhere very special, don't we, Mickey?." And in an instant the four of them coupled off, arm in arm, and began to walk away in the opposite direction from
Christopher. "Oi, squirt – I don't think we'll be needing this after all," said Terry, and he tossed the bat disdainfully over his shoulder onto the rocks below them. Just then it started to rain. "Oh dear," said Terry. "Got an umbrella, girls?"

"Does it look like we have?"

"Well we know just the place, don't we, Mickey boy? There's a bus shelter just across the road. Tucked away behind the trees, it's…. what's the word, Mickey?"

"Private, Terry."

"That's it, Corporal. Private."

"Sounds nice," said the taller girl.

"Then let us escort you…"

Christopher watched them walk away, then jumped down to pick up his bat. It was broken, right at the point where the handle joined the blade. He'd have to try and fix it before his grandfather saw it.

He turned towards home and wondered whether his Nanna would be back yet from his Auntie Florrie's. With luck she'd have stayed for a cup of tea, and he would be back before she realised he'd been gone. What would he do about his wet clothes, though? For the rain was now bouncing off the road.

The answer came soon enough. Just as he turned into the road where his grandparents lived, he saw his grandmother waiting in the porch. "Where've *you* been, my lad? I've been worried sick. I came back from Florrie's and you weren't here, not even a note, you could have been kidnapped for all I knew, then you turn up looking like a drowned rat. Where've you been anyway? No, don't tell me – I can see – you've got your cricket bat with you – you've been playing with Michael, haven't you? I thought you were supposed to be poorly, eh? Too poorly for chapel, but fit enough to play cricket. Well, you ought to be ashamed of yourself. Not only have you worried me half to death, but you've lied to your Grandfather. How do you think that's going to make him feel? Honestly, Christopher, he asks nothing of you, but you know he likes you to go to chapel with him – is that too much to ask?"

"No, Nanna. I'm sorry."

"Oh, it's easy to say you're sorry now, isn't it, but the damage is done. And you can stop your crying right now. Crying's not going to do you any good. I'll give you something to really cry about in a minute. Now get to your room, change out of those wet things, and think about what you've done."

*

The next morning the rain had stopped. The sun streamed through the curtains, waking Christopher from an empty, dreamless sleep. He got up and looked out of the window. As usual, the blackbird was sitting on the window-sill, almost as if he had been waiting.

"I shan't see you after tomorrow. Back to home and back to school."

He yawned and stretched. He felt all right, surprisingly, as though the emotions of yesterday had left him completely drained. He went into the kitchen where his grandmother was frying bacon. He knew that no more would be said about it.

"Sleep well?"

"Yes, thanks."

"Good lad. Here," she added, putting a plate of bacon sandwiches in front of him, "this'll put hairs on your chest."

After a while, his grandfather came in from the allotment at the back of his garden. "Nice morning, Christopher. What are your plans?"

"I don't have any."

"What? No plans on your last full day here?"

"Well – I thought I'd wait to see what you two were doing."

Hubert looked at Annie, who smiled and then turned away back to the sink. "Are you not playing cricket? It's a fine day for it."

"But what about you? Don't you have to go into Llandudno this morning? Maybe I could go with you?"

"Oh, I'm only going to the bank. That's not much fun for you, is it? No – you go and see if Michael's about. I expect he'll be waiting for you."

"Are you sure?"

"Well," said his grandmother, "if you'd rather stay here with me, I'm sure I could find some chores for you…"

"No thanks." Laughing, Christopher ducked under her outstretched, soapy arms and headed for the porch, where he saw his cricket bat – the special one his Granddad had made for him – lying against the door, and he stopped. "Granddad, have you got any string?"

"I expect so. Now what would you want that for?"

"Oh – I thought… I thought I'd bind it round the handle - like Gary Sobers does."

"Well if that's how Gary Sobers has it," said Granddad, smiling, "you'd best do the same. Follow me. There'll be some string in the shed, I shouldn't wonder."

Five minutes later Christopher was walking down the drive, opening the gate, then heading towards the passageway that led up to Michael's house. Just before he reached it, however, he stopped and sat on the wall. What if Michael doesn't want to see him, he thought? What if Terry's hanging around? What if they start teasing him again?

"Penny for them?"

"What?"

"Your thoughts." It was Julie. The girl from across the

126

way. "You looked miles away."

"I will be soon. I'm going back tomorrow."

"That's a shame. But you'll be back at half term, won't you? That's not long, is it? Six weeks? My mum says I can have a Halloween party. Would you like to come?"

Christopher shrugged. "Maybe."

"You're funny." Then she smiled at him sideways and pecked him on the cheek.

Christopher's jaw practically hit the floor.

"What's up? Never been kissed before? How about a proper one?"

Christopher's face went the colour of beetroot.

"I'm not going to ask you twice!"

"No thank you."

"Suit yourself." Julie jumped down from the wall about to go.

"Sorry," said Christopher. She paused and looked at him.

"Maybe at Halloween?" he offered.

She laughed, then sat back on the wall. "Who's your favourite Beatle?"

"John," he answered as quick as a flash.

"Is that 'cos he wears glasses like you?"

"No," he blushed again. "It's because…"

"Mine's Paul," she said quickly.

"Michael's middle name is Paul."

"Is it?" said Julie. "How interesting…" She smiled slowly to herself. "Well, I've got to go. Till Halloween then," and she stuck out her hand for him to shake in an oddly formal way.

Christopher went to take it. "Till Halloween. See you."

"Not if I see you first!" And she pulled her hand away at the last moment before running off across the street.

Christopher jumped down from the wall and walked on past Michael's house. He decided he wouldn't call on him just now. If Michael really wanted to see me, he thought, then let him come to me. He swung his bat over his shoulder and whistled as he walked on towards the beach. Suddenly a voice stopped him short.

"Can *I* come?" It was Michael, leaning out of his

upstairs window.

"I suppose. But just you – not Terry."

"Terry's working, remember? His holiday job in Llandudno,
deck chair attendant. "Are you going to the beach or the field?"

"The field's best, it's a truer wicket."

"D'you think it'll take spin today?"

"Might do. After the rain last night."

"Yeah. A real sticky dog."

Christopher stopped and turned to face Michael directly. "I've got my granddad's bat with me. We fixed it. If you want to play, you'll have to use that."

"Of course. That's great." They looked at each other. "Sorry about yesterday – it was Terry, he…"

"Forget it. Come on, it's my last full day today. Let's make the most of it."

"Bags I be Sobers?"

"All right. Are you bowling left arm fast, or googlies and chinamen?"

"That'd be telling. Who are you going to be? Ken Barrington? Tom Graveney?"

"No. I know exactly who I'm going to be."

"Who's that then, Chris?" asked Michael as he tossed the cricket ball from one hand to the other.

"Me," said Christopher, and they ran off towards the field, with the high white clouds scudding across blue skies on the last full day of the holidays. But they didn't care about that. They had all the time in the world.

Water Features 3

Peel '74
circling the ruined castle
the eye of the storm

we howl to the waves
here we all are, do your worst
young, invincible

4

Entering the Frame

Guilty Pleasures

I must have spent a thousand hours
in darkened cinemas - such guilty pleasures
especially in the afternoons,

such profligate waste, such indulgence
when you know you should be in the fresh air
doing something useful and you can still hear

your grandmother's voice chastising you
'haven't you anything better to do?' -
but when the lights begin to dim

and you hear once more the familiar strain
of MGM or Pearl & Dean
there's really only one answer:

over the rainbow lies buried treasure
and the place you're travelling to is home.

Pathé News:

Palaces of Dreams

5 – 4 – 3 – 2 - 1
on the screen a flickering cockerel crows -
a prelude to the Pathé Newsreel signature tune -
then a swinging iron bar demolishes
a cinema as it smashes
into its 1930's edifice…
Headline: Final Cinema in Trafford To Close

(Pathé Announcer: Voice Over):

> Trafford, named after the ancient De
> Trafford family, combines the former
> market towns of Sale and Altrincham,
> Stretford, Urmston and Partington, as
> well as several smaller neighbour-
> hoods, including *Old* Trafford, where
> the football and cricket grounds are.
> There's Denis Law, painted as a mural
> on a factory wall. And here's the
> cricket ball that Jack Duckworth once
> smacked for six all the way to London.
> (You don't believe it? Ask this old
> boy – he was there when he did it!)
>
> Trafford - just 40 square miles yet,
> when writer Chris Fogg was a boy –
> yes, that's him, with the Wyatt Earp
> hat - there were 20 cinemas there, and
> Chris reckons he visited every one.
>
> The first to be recorded was The Great
> American Bioscope, part of a
> travelling fair at Hale Moss in 1900.
> Just a minute - isn't that Great
> Grandmama holding on to her hat?
> She's been watching *Fred Karno's
> Circus*, I shouldn't wonder. And who's
> that cheeky chappie queueing up to
> take a peek at What the Butler Saw? It

must be Uncle Cyril...

Now there are none. A few remain in
different guises – a roundabout, a
supermarket, a scrap yard – these one-
time palaces of dreams...

the screen fades, the curtains close
we wait in vain for further cockerel crows...

The Last Picture Show
(Cinemas of Trafford)

The Central – converted from the former Clarion
Club - "every lady accompanied by a gentleman
FREE" - later the People's Palace,
or Flea Pit, so forced to close…

The Hippodrome – with tip-up seats in the Dress Circle -
"for easy passage with nothing to interrupt
your view" of a screen that could only fit '-inemascop…'

during the Blitz the blast of a bomb
swung the image to an adjacent wall
showing the full picture for the one and only time…

The New Electric Theatre – opened in 1914
with a separate side entrance "for the cheaper seats"
it showed footage from the Western
Front - and very little afterwards…

Hale Cinema – with its mock Tudor frontage
and "full augmented orchestra"
and, afterwards, "dancing in the Lounge" -
it burned down after a screening of *The Towering Inferno*

The Regal – "a cathedral of cinemas" -
two thousand seats and five thousand lights
that twinkled in time to the Wurlitzer

organ that rose from under the orchestra
pit to fountains of Dancing Waters
like a scene from the *Arabian Nights*

The Pyramid – an early Egyptian
theme park with usherettes
dressed as Nefertiti
and its own in-house telephone reception –
"This is PYR 123…" –

as the Pyramid Orchestra
played live *The Entrance of Cleopatra*
(portrayed by Manchester's Mary Thornley
All England's première senior danseuse)

and the Lido Singers – Winnie & Hilda
A Song, A Smile & A See-Saw -
sang on stage three times nightly
before *Movietone News* and *Mickey Mouse*

The Sale Palace – converted back
from a "high class roller rink" on
the "best American principles", its fake
30's frontage a boardwalk
of a Western Cowboy Saloon

The Savoy - "our Cinema-de-Luxe
showing all-electric animated pics
suitable for all ages…"

sapphire-blue curtains, mahogany panels,
foyer filled with white marble
statues - its final film, *Holiday on the Buses*…

The Corona, The Globe and *The Trafford* -
afterwards a car park, a scrap yard,
and a plot of disused warehouses

for a time becoming the depot
for Manchester's Carriage & Tramways Co -
home for more than three thousand horses –
all now gone for good…

The Longford –
later a mortuary, then shut

The Lyceum –
the "Bug Hut"
or "lie *down* and see 'em"

The Imperial Picture Palace –
"the Brooks Bar Bollywood" –
all-singing, all-dancing Cottonopolis…

The Essoldo –
formerly *The Futurist* -
when the house lights started to dim
its satin-ruched drapes would glow

wrapping you in a warm blanket
enfolding you in a deep forest
fire of red and green and apricot
a glittering Guy Fawkes Night light

The Picture Drome –
(affectionately known
as the "Ranch House")
for it only showed Westerns

and finally the three in Urmston
the three that I went to the most -
The Palace, The Empress, The Curzon

The Palace – squeezed beneath a railway
arch - would shake, rattle and roll
to the clattering trains above us

home of the Saturday Matinee
the mad dash for the front row
like the scramble for Africa

Flash Gordon and *The Lone Ranger*
where we'd gallop our horses up and down aisles
whoopin' and hollerin' and diving for cover
from the usherette – my best friend's older sister –

sometimes, when sitting on the benches,
eyes on the screen, a sweet half-way to our mouths,
she'd stealthily creep upon us

with a window-pole, towel-wrapped tight to one end,
which she'd stretch along the front row's length
to whack the backs of our heads…

The Empress – green and gold
with its dome like a mosque's
and its penchant for holy epics

The Ten Commandments, Ben Hur,
King of Kings, Samson & Delilah
Barabas, The Robe, Solomon & Sheba
The Greatest Story Ever Told

– torn down like the temple to make way
for a *Tesco* with no Charlton Heston
to hold back the Pharaohs or part the Red Sea

and, last but not least, *The Curzon* –
with blue butterflies on its gold curtains
and back-row double-seats for courting couples
(where I snogged Susan Holmes through *Gone With The Wind*

"Can I see you again?" I ask as the last bus pulls
in, - the night seems ablaze, like Atlanta.
"Well I'm sure I don't know," she replies with a grin.
"Tomorrow *is* another day…")

and now it's another day for *The Curzon* too -
the final cinema in Trafford to close
Mamma Mia and *Hellboy 2* -
the gold curtains came down for the last
time and the blue butterflies folded their wings

(on stage a ghostly couple sings –
echoes of my parents from earlier days –
Have You Seen My Lady…?
The Boy I Love Is Looking Down On Me…)

and the last two patrons to leave
had, flustered, returned to retrieve

a forgotten scarf and a last look round
at its darkening, empty art-deco surrounds…

The Last Picture Show

The First Film I Ever Saw

The first film I ever saw was *Bambi* -
I must have been five -
my mum and gran took me,
perhaps it was my birthday.
People stamped their feet and chanted
'We want the film, we want the film'
and a half-eaten bun landed on my gran's lap
which she wouldn't let me eat -
then the lights went down and it all went still
and I was... traumatised!

No one had prepared me for this:
suddenly it went from cute bunnies
and 'kind of wobbly, ain't he?'
to forest fires and the death of Bambi's mom
to loss and separation, metaphors for
Hitler's advancing hordes,
the need for self-sacrifice... and I thought -
if this is cinema, give me real life any time,
Disney, America – who needs them...?
I didn't go again for two years

Then it was another fairy tale -
The Wizard of Oz - and wouldn't you know it,
just when you thought you knew where you were -
Kansas, Aunt Em, Toto and Dorothy –
suddenly there was a tornado
and you were whisked away
to munchkins and tin men and talking lions
and poppy fields where if you fell asleep
you never woke up and a wizard and...
well, that's a horse of a different colour...

But worse than any of this was the witch
who captured Toto and rode on a broomstick,
whose green face loomed out of the screen
and looked directly at me, just me, no one else:

'I'll get you, my pretty, and your little dog too!'
That was it - I was under the seat in a flash
and that's where I stayed, not coming out
till Dorothy clicked her ruby slippers, closed her eyes and said:
'There's no place like home, there's no place like home'
and we were back in the land of black-and-white again…

Vertical Hold

TV was safer
for a start it was in the living room
and you could always switch it off
though sometimes it could drive you mad
when the vertical hold went
and you had to hit the top of the set
or watch a person's legs
walking on top of his head

we didn't have one
but Pete's family did, next door -
we'd crowd round after school
to watch the latest episode
of *Thunderbirds, The Mysterons*
Supercar and *Stingray* -
"This is terrible, we're all going to be killed…"
not noticing the fixed grins or ridiculous strings -

then act it out
every day in the playground
till the following week and the next episode -
we spent half our lives speaking in American accents
even as RAF pilots winning the Battle of Britain
or when we were Dan Dare fighting against the Mekon -
America was in colour
we were black and white

then the Beatles came and changed the rules
they grew up on the same streets that we did
they spoke with the same accents we had
and sang about people we knew
places we'd remember though some might change

25 June 1967, 8.54pm: the day the earth stood still -
the first live satellite to transmit around the world
The Beatles sang *All You Need Is Love*
at the height of the Vietnam War
and the Klan burned their records
on Alabama bonfires…

Fatal Attraction

I've started watching more and more old British movies – World War II escape dramas, Ealing Comedies, early Powell & Pressburger. I am finding their black and white certainties so reassuring just at this moment in my life, and I'm not sure why. Greer Garson saving the day as Mrs Miniver, the recently widowed Patricia Roc pluckily smiling through at the close of *Millions Like Us*, the whole village of Bramley End coming together to thwart a Nazi invasion in *Went the Day Well*, Wendy Hiller so cocksure she knows *exactly* where she's going, the absolute certainty of David Niven's love for Kim Hunter that truly is *A Matter of Life and Death*. Even the brasher new wave of the early 60's – Laurence Harvey in R*oom at the Top*, Alan Bates in *A Kind of Loving*, Albert Finney in *Saturday Night & Sunday Morning*, each of them taking on the establishment – *"all the rest is propaganda"* – and losing – even *they* carry with them a clear-eyed conviction that seems so appealing just now when everything seems in flux, so uncertain, on the cusp of permanent change.

They throw a light on a lost age, the post-war privations, the never-had-it-so-good 50's, times that, when they were actually happening and we were living through them, felt far from attractive – a sense of cocooned privilege and rank that was simply waiting for the likes of Brando and Dean to come along and smash their old world order. "What are you rebelling against?" they were asked. "What've you got?" they'd insolently reply. We were all of us back then secure in our belief that we could be contenders, somebody.

So what has happened? The 1960's came along and swept away many of those old values for ever. Not for nothing is that decade so inextricably linked with different modes of liberation – social, economic, political, sexual; it's also a decade that we still see vividly in colour, after the previous drab decades of black and white austerity. I still look back on those times, the 60's – such formative times for me – with affection, nostalgia and excitement, the sense that suddenly anything and everything was possible.

So why this current fixation with those older, duller, safer worlds? How can I both see through them for the falsehoods they proffered, and yet at the same time be so emotionally drawn back towards them, to wish, almost, that I could have lived back then myself, fully inhabiting them? I watch them now and they seem to me to be depicting a sort of home I never actually knew but which I somehow recognise and crave.

This fascination exerts a surprisingly strong pull over me, even though I can stand back, as I watch these films, quite appalled by the lack of complexity and ambiguity, or by the inflexible rigidity of a class system in which everyone so clearly (and acceptingly, it seems) knows their place – until Joe Lampton steps off that train in Warnley, that is, in search of a clean shirt and a good time.

Maybe in the end, like all cinema, it is about make-believe, pretence – like Michael Redgrave in *The Captive Heart*, pretending to be Rachel Kempson's dead, feckless husband, returning home from war a better person, the man her husband could and should have been – and that it is this suggestive sleight of hand that lures us in, unwitting accomplices to preserve the status quo. Such certainties, such moral absolutes, particularly in times of change and upheaval such as the ones we are living through today, can seem dangerously, seductively attractive, so that Celia Johnson, at the end of *Brief Encounter*, can be overwhelmed with grief as Trevor Howard takes his unspoken, final leave of her, but at the same time, as the steam on the station from his departing train at last evaporates, the speck in her eye has gone too; she can see clearly that she must return home to her husband, her quiet sacrifice quite truly heroic. Perhaps in their way it is *these* films – not the new wave of angry young men brought to us by Lindsay Anderson, John Schlesinger and Karel Reiz – that are the true subversives? And that makes me feel uncomfortable.

Meanwhile, I make a cup of tea, reach for a packet of ginger nuts and (while rain has stopped play at the cricket) put *Kind Hearts & Coronets* onto the DVD player, *"revelling in all the exuberance of the period with none of the concomitant crudity..."*

Black & White

crashing on the sofa to watch old black & white movies
I Know Where I'm Going springs to mind –
except that I don't…

Test Cards

Do you remember test cards –
bars of black and white pigment,
later strips of colour, they
contained a set of patterns
enabling television
cameras and receivers to
show the picture correctly?

In the centre was a young
girl playing noughts and crosses
on a chalk board with her toy
clown – for thirty years her face
was on TV for several
hours of every day, is still
the most aired face in British
television history,
once mischievously replaced
by Daleks from Doctor Who.

Now she passes by unseen,
all but forgotten, unknown
along with *The Potter's Wheel*,
those treasured intermissions,
brief pauses between programmes,
horses ploughing open fields
beneath wide vast skies, *River
and Birds, Windmill, Angel Fish,
Prunella the White Kitten,
Sea and Rocks, Loch Reflections,*
never forgetting *London
to Brighton in Four Minutes* –
all on YouTube now of course
should you care to look them up…

Modern test cards now include
calibrated colour bars
allowing chroma and tint

to be finely adjusted,
infinite hues minutely
tuned to register
every shade of the spectrum
including analogue black,
blacker than black and full white,
but we never see them now,
they're no longer transmitted,
have become invisible
like memories.

I recall
how they were accompanied
sometimes by a high-pitched whine,
a screaming howl of protest,
so that when you switched the set
off, the picture would collapse
into a small white circle
in the centre of the screen,
a hole sucking all the light
around deep into its core,
leaving an image that stayed
long, long after it had gone
burning the retina's back...

Summer Holiday

summer
1963
Sunday afternoon
I'm 11

for a birthday treat
my mum and dad take me
over the water
across the canal
to Manchester –
bright lights and a movie
ABC Deansgate
'Home of Cinerama'
I'm beside myself

(though to be honest
early Cinerama's a bit dodgy
it wraps around you –
I'm reminded of curtains?
floor-to-ceiling
horse-shoe bay window
the sort my grandma had –
three separate sections
you can see the joins where they meet
with a couple of gaps in between
so the image doesn't…
                              quite…
                                        fit)

still –
it was new
modern –
like me
the only trouble is
my parents haven't told me
which film we'll be seeing
it's a surprise, they say
(covering my eyes)

"Surprise!"
(so I can't see the posters)
"Coming to a cinema near you!"

such enticement
my excitement's
growing by the minute
rising by the second –
which is not necessarily a good idea…

two years before
after I'd pestered and pleaded for weeks
my mum finally took me to The Gaumont
poshest cinema of all –
grand sweeping staircase
crystal chandelier
carved Cupid columns
fabric moquette wallpaper –
to see *The Lone Ranger Meets Tonto*
complete with a real cowboy
live on stage
lassoing like a rodeo

Hi
        Oh
                Silver
                        Away

I was excited then too
so excited I threw up
all over the usherette
while queuing for a Kia-Ora…

but that was two years ago
I'm 11 now
a big boy
going to the Grammar School

finally
the curtains open –

plush green velvet
gold brocaded tassels –
and my heart…
                    sinks
                              like a stone

Cliff Richard?
Summer Holiday?

I can't believe it
my parents think they're being 'with it'
but they're so missing the mark

two weeks before
in a tent at Urmston Show
on Chassen Park
where every Sat'day I play football
The Beatles had played –
it cost 12/6
(five weeks pocket money)
I couldn't afford it, so…

Pete went though
my next door neighbour –
his favourite bit?
when John sang:
She Loves You Shit, Shit, Shit

but Cliff Richard –
he's so lame
so wet
so safe –
and what's even worse
when the picture starts
it's in black and white –
black and white?!

Still
much as I hate Cliff
I love the cinema more

so —

I sink back
low into my seat
suck my Kia-Ora
through a straw-rer
and drown
deep in the warm
                luxurious

                        waters

                                of Cinerama…

then —
looming out of the grey
omnipresent
monochrome
up there on the screen
the bleached out cityscape
bomb sites, waste land and demolition
I walk through every day
suddenly
there appears…
a big…
        bright…
                red double-decker bus!

at first
I think my eyes are playing tricks
that they're only seeing what they want to
but no —

there it is again
colour after colour
shade upon shade
a whole rainbow spectrum
spreading across the screen
glorious Technicolor
magic marker
child's colouring book
a perfect, pristine tin of Winsor & Newton Paints

a dazzling *red* double-decker bus
transporting me to a future that belongs…

                                        only…
                                            to me

I tune out Cliff
imagining instead
a different song
with different words
sung with hard northern voices
in accents I can understand
blazing a trail through landscapes
I can truly call my own

this imagined
                other
                        version of myself
stands beside me
shoulder to shoulder
the two of us striding off
towards a bright, new dawn…

"You and I have memories
Longer than the road that stretches out ahead…"
                        (Two of Us: Lennon/McCartney)

Home Movies

shadows dance in black and white on kitchen walls
projected through Venetian blinds
long lost home movies found in dusty attics
sepia memories

The Aliens Have Landed

1951
The Year My Parents Got Married

(the same weekend that the Festival of
Britain
opened along the South Bank -
The Far Tottering and Oyster Creek Railway
The Lion & Unicorn Pavilion
The Skylon Tower and Dome of Discovery
(nicknamed the "flying saucer")

1951
The Year Of Living Dangerously

Tories Re-Elected!
Churchill Razes Festival Site –
New Homes Shall Arise From The Slums!

but not on The Bama
another forty years would pass
before *they* were cleared –

boarded up, abandoned
the steel works closed down
the big ships no longer sailed

down the alley, alley-o
though children still sang of them
rope-skipping their way down the years…

Alabama –
Choctaw for scorched earth…

*

My parents met in Manchester
in the rooms of Madame Hedevari
a Jewish-Hungarian emigrée
who'd fled the tanks in Budapest
who'd once appeared with Caruso
and who now taught my parents to sing…

My father, who every evening
when he came home from work
from the local asbestos factory
would sing a snatch of Puccini
to wipe away the day
Ché Gelida Manina...

My mother, who looked like Marie Lloyd
who "wanted-to-go-to-Birmingham-
but-they've-taken-me-off-to-Crewe"
who told me the story of *Treasure Island*
every day when she walked me to school
acting out all of the parts...

*

```
1951
Movie News

Brando Scorches In Streetcar Sizzler!
(Blanche may have depended upon the kindness
of strangers
but HUAC urges the naming of names)

Jimmy Stewart Scores Hit With Harvey!
(the pink-eyed invisible six-foot rabbit
that nobody sees but Jimmy -

                         like the
pinkies that only McCarthy could see
but who testified all the same)

Bedtime With Bonzo!
(where future President Reagan
is upstaged by a chimp -
life will imitate art...)
and The Day The Earth Stood Still - Dark
Alien Spacecraft Lands in New York!
(starring the Robot, Gort)
```

*

My parents went to the cinema
often, once or twice a week
(mostly to *The Curzon*,
sometimes to *The Empress*)
I don't know if they saw these
or not – it was before I was born –
though there were others I'm sure they'd
have gone to. *A Place in the Sun*,
An American In Paris, David & Bathsheba,
The African Queen, Showboat –
transatlantic culture clashes –

but *The Day The Earth Stood Still*
I *know* they saw, though it wasn't till
years later, on TV…
                              I came in towards
the end from cricket and dad gestured
me to sit: it's good is this,
he said, but I've missed the start,
I argued, I won't get it, yes
you will, he said, and he was right…

Movie mogul Zanuck,
when asked about casting for Klaatu,
is said to have puffed out his chest,
bit on his cigar and, looking
straight to camera, remarked:
"Who else would you get to play an alien?
A Brit, of course!"
                              (Michael Rennie,
later to track down dinosaurs in *The Lost World*,
lands his spacecraft in a different, but just as hostile,
jungle).
          "Hell, he even tries to claim
he's one of us, passes himself off
as a regular guy, gets to date
Patricia Neale, a real looker,
and then he has the nerve
to try and lecture us,
he sends this robot –

Gort, the 'ultimate weapon' –
to stand guard while he speaks,
otherwise we'd've nuked him –
better if we had, I say..."

*

We squeeze together on the green moquette settee
as if we're hunched up in the front stalls
of the Empress or the Curzon
half-expecting the usherette to glide backwards
between us, her wares displayed -
Kia-Ora, Choc Ices, Lyon's Maid...
I shut my eyes, imagining the adverts
(with curtains closed against the sun)
the cartoons, trailers, newsreels
my mum and dad transfixed on either side of me...

The Day The Earth Stood Still

Cue the film's climactic closing moments
when KLAATU reveals himself at last, confronts

us with questions we'd rather not face –
GORT beside him, his expression ice...

KLAATU speaks

to the world's assembled delegation –
military leaders, the United Nations,

presidents, popes and law enforcers,
a battery of ranked TY reporters.

He talks about the imperative for
security for all, or no one is secure;

he tells us we have always known this,
that our forefathers knew instinctively

when they made their laws to govern us
and hired policemen to enforce them –

this does not mean giving up freedom
except the freedom to act responsibly...

*KLAATU indicates beside him GORT
who unflinchingly, unblinkingly stares out*

*blank and impassive, his massive size
casting down dark and lengthening shadows*

KLAATU speaks:

"We have created a race of robots
whose function is to patrol the planets

and preserve the peace of the universe,
ceded them absolute power over us.

At the first sign of aggression
they will act at once, elimination

leaving the rest of us, the best of us,
free, free from fear, free to pursue

more profitable enterprises –
you scratch our backs, we'll protect you...

KLAATU smiles:

"It may not be perfect but it works,
this mutual accommodation,

so join us and live in peace,
or pursue your present course

and face certain obliteration:
you decide, the choice is yours.

We will be waiting for your answer..."
The lights from the alien spacecraft glimmer,

shimmer, in the day the earth stood still,
as the screen fades to black and credits roll...

*

And *as* the credits roll my dad nods,
goes towards the piano and with
his right hand picks out Puccini –
my mum's fists are balled like she's been
given the black spot by Blind Pew -
Gort's eyeless visage lingers…
Questa Quella…

        this or that…

                which…?

        *

Woody Allen once famously said:
"Why do they re-make all the *good* films?
It's the *bad* films they should make again,
that would be the smarter thing…"

When Ian McKellen re-made *Richard III*
the previews were less than encouraging.
"I don't get it – Richard *3*?
What happens in Richards 1 and 2?
Do I need to see those first? And –
just an idea – why not call it *Ricky 3*?
You know – like *Rocky*? That would jive…"

But still they do it, don't they?
Did you *see* the recent remake of *The Day The Earth Stood Still*?
You didn't? Can't say I blame you. Leave well alone.
To begin with they broke the cardinal rule of casting:
they replaced Michael Rennie with Keanu Reeves –
who is NOT A BRIT!

Now, if they'd cast Keanu as Gort,
that might have played better…

Vicarious

I seem to live each day by proxy
through music, movies, books,
experiencing the roller coaster
of other people's journeys
more than my own which takes,
it seems, a back seat always,
my default position to tell
stories and incidents from my past,
anecdotes ever so slightly
embroidered to raise a smile
here, elicit a response
there, sometimes I almost
think I've lived even a dull
approximation of that experience

but in art it's all so different,
frequently it stops me in my tracks -
I walk into a gallery of Rothkos
and at once am overwhelmed with tears,
or when Tess's note is pushed beneath
Angel's *rug* as well as his door,
or Miles Davis playing *Blue in Green* -
each of these contains a moment
so intense, so heightened, it unlocks
a door once opened I never want to close
evoking longings, dreams, fears
not embodied in real life

and it's not just art - if anything
cheap sentiment is worse,
an unlikely happy ending,
small acts of self-sacrifice
or, especially, when somebody is *nice*,
the slightest thing unhinges me -
in movies I've learned how to feel,

how to react, how to behave,
things I can't translate to what is real,
which always seems to matter less -
I've heard the mermaids singing
and though they haven't sung for me
I keep on listening just in case
the anaesthetic's wearing off

for even these old songs and films
are from a former bygone day -
I can't relate to *now*, it seems -
Astaire dancing cheek to cheek,
Garland lighting up the screen
lamenting the man who got away,
Chet Baker's funny valentine
who despite having a physique
(like mine) that's somewhat less than Greek
implores me still to stay -
I'm not such a fool,
I never did, never will, possess
Gable's charm, or Kelly's grace,
Flynn's dash, or Bogart's cool

but something keeps pulling me back
(like the bracelet on Barbara Stanwyck's
ankle in *Double Indemnity*)
the promise and allure
of a life fully lived, not
filtered down vicariously
or played safe, but on the edge,
reckless, without fear or shame -
humankind, we're told, cannot bear
very much reality but
the dvd seems permanently
on pause - either I'm
going to walk through that door, or watch
the re-run for the umpteenth time...

Cut

(NYC – first trip)

It's like stepping into a movie
(Woody Allen, Scorsese)
everything feels so familiar -
the Sikh cab driver, the pretty young
girl I share the ride with from JFK
who tells me her life story
who gives me her number
who asks me to come up and see her
some time as we drop her off near
the drug store - *you are now entering
Queen's* - then across the East River
(*I could've been a contender*)
I'm on such a high five roll
that even when you don't appear

to meet me as arranged I just call
from the phone booth on the corner
like I've seen a thousand times before
in God knows how many film noir
scenes and when you're not there
to pick up I know just what to do -
take the subway up to Herald Square
ride the elevator right on
up to the top of the Empire
State (*An Affair to Remember*) when
before I've even reached a couple
of blocks I walk smack right into you -
they couldn't script this - best to quit
before some director calls out 'Cut!'

5

Coming of Age

Rites of Passage

(Cadishead 1963)

Behind the schoolyard, between the steel works
and the embankment, lay the bomb-site:
a ruin of mattresses, heaped bricks, dumped tyres;
a tangle
of wrecked cars, bed-springs, rusty wires.
Into this jungle
we boys plunged, to smoke and write
rude words about the gaudy girls
who coiled their fingers round their curls
and taunted us with threats of sex –

blown kisses, flashed knickers – then a shriek
as they fled towards the railway track
to blow away time on dandelion clocks,
their laughter
stinging us like electric shocks.
After
these preliminaries came the ac-
-tual initiation rite
itself – a dare? a fight? –
spilling blood to join their clique.

When my turn came I had to walk across
a plank suspended over a lime pit
where rats the size of tom-cats lurked –
you scored
extra if it bounced or jerked.
My reward,
if ever I dared to do it,
was to be ceremonially led,
blindfold, towards the cycle shed
where waiting for me was Margaret Ness.

Margaret, Margaret Ness, whose dimpled cheeks, shy smile
broke a hundred hearts. My classmate George
and I fought for her through a whole playtime,
dislodging
the stacked coke-pile till she came
watching
us with a look I couldn't gauge...
Then one week after finishing school
George drowned in a crowded swimming pool -
I read it in *The Daily Mail.*

*

The steel works shut down. There are no bomb-sites
now. The school's all boarded up. Weeds clog
the playground. I've not seen Margaret since.
Finding
years later our initials on a fence
reminded
me: the past looks different when it's dug
up. Like archaeologists we pin on names,
misinterpret the unearthed remains,
best left covered by the new estates.

Saturday Mornings

("*Tic-tac is a traditional method of signs used by bookmakers to communicate the odds of certain horses. Tic-tac men would wear white gloves to allow their hand movements to be easily seen over wide distances across the racecourse.*"
Wikipedia).

1

Saturday mornings meant
running bets for my dad
to the local bookie's round the corner
when betting was barely legal
so you had to use a pseudonym –

my father, Eric, chose *Enrico*
(after Caruso) which made somehow
the gambling seem more glamorous
a far cry from grandma's dire warnings
delivered daily like a sermon

*… first it's a shilling, then it's a pound,
then it's the whole house…*

her hands rising to her face in horror
a gesture a Geisha might make
delicate, rehearsed, designed to deter
but I was in thrall to the litany
of betting slips clutched in hot hands

*they're under starter's orders…
… and they're off*

yankee each way treble accumulator
in letters spilling unconfined
beyond pre-drawn lines on Basildon Bond
blue carbon paper placed beneath
for copies he always kept

*

(every week would see the same routine)

- you're too young
- it's not for me, it's my dad
- it says Enrico, how do I know that isn't you?
- I'd be Camille
- our secret then…

(like father, like son)

2

(like father, like son)
I studied the form
The Sporting Life and *Chronicle*

compiling vital statistics
picking winners for the week ahead
recorded in red exercise books

with the old weights and measures
imperial dry, avoirdupois, long or lineal
listed on the back –

two links one chain
ten chains one furlong
eight furlongs one mile

furlongs the measurement of racing
that could all come down to half a length
a neck, short head, dead heat

bushels and pecks, fathoms and leagues
rods, poles and perches
(I never did learn what *they* were for)

*

each day en route for school
crossing the Ship Canal
I'd stop to swap tips with the Irish navvies

my grandma needn't have worried
it was never the money for me
more the pleasure in picking winners

working out odds signalled in code
tic-tac men like Masons
black bowler hats, white kid gloves

silent scriptures in the sky
I longed to learn their language
like my granddad's semaphore

fifteen to eight, a hundred to thirty
even money the favourite
twenty to one - bar...

I raced to the bookie's
the following Saturday
to try out my new-learned skill

to my delight he signalled me back –
I still need your father's slip, he called
Enrico... Camille... each way...

3

but soon gambling was commonplace
nom de plumes discarded
we got a telephone – 2587 party line –
and my dad rang in his bets
(though he'd always begin *Enrico here*...)

and I stopped reading *The Sporting Life*
switched my interest from horses to girls
whose vital statistics I sought out in inches
while weights and measures went metric
(twenty grains equal one scruple)

Water Features 4

'77
Lindisfarne – water lapping
the narrow causeway

vanished in seconds
I put my foot on the gas
it's now or never

Wibbersley Park

My grandmother was the third of ten children, eight of whom survived. She was born the daughter of a miner in Ellen Brook, close to Chat Moss, but when she was still just a girl, the family moved across the other side of the Moss to Irlam in a three bedroom terraced house on Astley Road, and her father became a labourer at the local tar works. She was christened Esther Hannah after each grandmother, whom they visited on alternate Sundays. This necessitated her parents having to remember to call her by the appropriate grandmother's name, depending upon which one they happened to be with, and this proved too much for her exasperated father. "From now on, we're calling her Annie, and let that be an end of it," he'd said, so from that day on she was known by all as Annie, later as Auntie Annie to the literally dozens of nieces and nephews (plus other less connected children) who came her way.

So when her elder sister Ethel decided she wanted to emigrate to Canada, it was to Annie she turned to for advice as to how she might best appease her father. When "our Tilly", as Mathilda, the youngest girl in the family, was universally known, suddenly announced that she was considering adopting her middle name Laurie as what she would prefer to be known by, it was to Annie she confided first, and it was Annie who made sure that none of the others attempted to tease her. She was a tigress, too, when it came to protecting Stanley. Stanley was a little slow; he never went to school and he never learned to read or write. But woe betide any other street kid who dared to make fun of him. It was she who encouraged him in his love of animals and, especially, in the rare gift he proved to possess with birds: he nursed them, ringed them, later bred them. Stanley was the middle of three brothers who survived infancy (with David and George, the twins, dying when they were just a few days old). Jim was the eldest, named after his father, and Annie hero-worshipped him, as did her closest sister, Edith; while Harry, the youngest, was hot-headed with a fiery temper. Many was the time when Annie would intervene to save Harry from himself.

She seemed earmarked for the role of carer from early

on, helping her mother with all these children who came after her, and generally looking after the household, from feeding and wringing the necks of chickens they kept in the back yard, (before plucking and cleaning out the innards, and then helping her mother to roast them), to cooking, cleaning, polishing and mending. While all her other siblings would leave the house one by one to work – in the Soap Works, Margarine Works, council offices, on the railways, at the printer's, on a farm – Annie stayed on at home. Except for once. When she was 13 she was asked to go and work up at the Big House in Worsley as a maid. She stayed just a month. Returning for her first day off, she was greeted by her family as if she had been lost at sea, and she simply didn't return. "She's needed here," her father said, and the matter was never spoken of again.

It was no surprise therefore that when the First World War broke out, when Annie was 17, she would volunteer as a V.A.D at nearby Wibbersley Park, a gracious house built by a Mr & Mrs Stott in the 1870's standing in its own modest grounds, which had been seconded for the duration to serve as a Military Hospital. Wibbersley Park was a few miles away in Flixton. This meant that she had to borrow her brother Jim's bike and cycle all the way to the Ship Canal, across the lock gates, then down to the ferry, a row boat which took people, bicycles and animals across to Flixton for a penny. Then it was a further mile's cycle up Irlam Road till she reached Wibbersley Park. Not being a trained nurse, she was initially used as a ward maid, cleaning up after the doctors and nurses had changed wound dressings, but it soon became clear that she was a natural carer and a quick learner, and before long she was being allowed to do more nursing duties, at which she quietly, unfussily excelled.

The day after war was declared, her brother Jim enlisted. He joined the Royal Scots Fusiliers because, he said, he wanted to wear a kilt, and he went up to Edinburgh for initial training and then was piped aboard the troop train, marching the length of Princes Street to thousands of cheering crowds. On his brief leave home before being posted to France, he had his photograph taken standing in full regalia behind Annie and Edith, modestly seated below in neat white blouses with enamelled brooches at their throats. I have this photograph above my desk as I am writing this down. In the spring of 1915 he was due a second leave. Annie was at home in Astley Road having just cycled back from her shift at Wibbersley Park and was resting on the settee in the parlour, the rarely used front room, when she heard the door open and in walked Jim. He put down his kit bag and perched on the arm of the settee.

"I hope you're taking good care of that bike of mine, our Annie," he said. "I shall be wanting it back after this show's over."

My grandmother told me this story about Jim when I was 10 years old. "I can't remember what it was I said back to him," she said, "but I usually gave as good as I got."

"Well," Jim went on, "I just want you to know that you needn't worry about it." She went suddenly quiet.

"What is it, Nanna?"

"I think I must have nodded off – I was always tired in the war – but the next thing I know there's a knocking at the front door. I got up to answer it, and there's this postman with a telegram. I knew straight away what it was. Jim had just come on ahead, to prepare me…"

The telegram baldly stated that Private James Eve of the Royal Scots Fusiliers had been killed in action on the first day of the 2nd Battle of Ypres, 21st April 1915.

His name is listed in the book of honour always kept open in Edinburgh Castle, and Annie and Edith travelled up to read it there after the war was over.

"Was that your brother's ghost?" I remember asking in wide-eyed wonder.

"I don't like the word 'ghost'," she replied. "That sounds frightening, and this wasn't frightening in the least. It was…" she paused, "like being tucked up with a blanket when you're not feeling well."

"I wish I could see a ghost," I said. "Then I could tell people at school all about it."

"You'll see the back of my hand," she said, "if you don't get out from under my feet. Now off you go into the fresh air. Unless you want me to give you some chores instead. There's always the brasses to polish." And away I would run…

After the war ended, the Stott family never returned to Wibbersley Park, and the house lay empty for years, falling into neglect until it was pulled down in 1925, and a dozen small semis were built on the land, plus a community hall, which for a time was a youth club. The Stotts retired to another gracious house, on Church Road, with a wild, overgrown orchard behind, the back of which was next door but one to where I lived after our family crossed over the water of the Ship Canal from Irlam. I used to climb the railings to play there with the other kids living nearby. Later, when I was a teenager, we all used to take a short cut through it up to the youth club at Wibbersley Park, not realising till my grandmother came to live with us after my granddad died, that this was the place where she had been a V.A.D.

*

Fast forward fifty years to May 1968. I'm a couple of months shy of 16 and it's a Saturday night. My grandmother still lives with us in a different house in Flixton. Near the station. About a mile and a half from Wibbersley. My friend Dave, who lives just round the corner, across the iron bridge, calls round one Saturday afternoon while I'm listening to the football results on the radio.

"Why don't you come round after tea?" he says. "Pat's bringing the new Beatles single." Pat was Dave's girlfriend and the new Beatles single was *Lady Madonna*. Dave knows I won't be able to resist that, and so, just after 7 o'clock, I cut through the cobbled back alley that runs from the iron bridge down the side of his house, slip over the wall and walk through his back door into their kitchen.

Mrs Randall is there, Dave's mum, standing by the kettle. "Hi, Chris. Just go straight into the front room. Dave said you might be coming round. They've got a surprise for you, I believe."

"Thanks, Mrs Randall. Dave said…"

"Did he now?" She turns away slightly, suppressing an amused smile. "Well, just make yourself at home. I'll bring in the tea in a minute."

From the front room I can already hear the strains of

Lady Madonna, Paul's honky tonk piano thumping through the closed door. "... *listen to the music playing in your head...*" I bound in, about to say something about how great it sounds, and then I see what Dave's mum means about the surprise, and I'm frozen to the spot.

"Hi, Chris," says Dave. "This is Sue."

And there, sitting on the sofa by the window, is this beautiful girl with shoulder-length dark hair, like a Madonna, but wearing a short black mini skirt and matching boots.

"Hello," I think I manage to stammer.

"Pleased to meet you," she replies instantly. She sounds confident and assured.

"She's a friend from school," says Pat helpfully. Pat lives in Irlam, across the canal, so that must mean Sue does too. I don't know any girls really, for the school I go to is all boys.

Lady Madonna has finished, and the hiss of the needle on the vinyl as the record keeps spinning round fills the sudden silence. "What do you think?" says Dave. I turn to him in panic. "The record, I mean. I'll play it again, shall I?"

At that moment Dave's mum breezes in with a tray. "The tea's brewing, and there's chocolate digestives. Are you alright, Chris? Why don't you sit down? There's plenty of room on the sofa."

"Thanks, Mrs Randall. I'm fine." Sue, I notice, has moved her handbag from the sofa, so that I can sit down beside her.

"Well, I'll just be in the back if you need anything. It's nearly time for *The Avengers*." And off she goes. Right now, I am wishing I could be there with her, watching Steed and Emma Peel, instead of here, and then it strikes me that Sue bears more than a passing resemblance to Diana Rigg. Does she do karate, I find myself wondering, as I sit on the sofa beside her? Just relax, I tell myself, it'll be fine.

Dave puts the record on again, while Pat pours the tea. "Sugar, Sue?"

"No thanks."

"Sweet enough," I say, before I can stop myself. Even though Dave has his back towards me, I can feel him rolling his eyes, but Sue just smiles, sweetly.

"Tuesday afternoon is never ending..." sings Paul.

"Which one are you?" asks Sue.

"Eh?"

"Which child?"

I must still look perplexed.

"What day were you born on?" she adds patiently.

"Oh, I see. Monday, I think."

" 'Monday's Child is fair of face'," she says, smiling.

"Chris is the exception that proves the rule," remarks Dave. I shoot him a look.

"What about you?" I ask.

"Saturday," she says, then starts to laugh. " 'Saturday's Child works hard for a living'!"

"Tell me about it," says Pat. They have both worked all day in their local supermarket, yet somehow have managed to arrive here this evening fresh, clean and shining. Whereas I, who don't have a Saturday job, look like I've been dragged through a hedge backwards.

"And we'll both be starting full time in a couple of months when we leave school," adds Sue.

I feel awkward, for Dave and I will be staying on.

Perhaps Dave feels the same, for he gets up to put on a different record – *Rain* – the 'B' side to *Paperback Writer*, while Pat gets up to pour the tea.

Outside it is raining quite hard. "Appropriate song," I say, trying to steer the conversation to a more neutral area, gesturing to the window.

I don't know why this wasn't the 'A' side," says Dave. "It's much the better track." He's right, and we all nod sagely. He flops back onto the armchair, and when she has finished pouring the tea, Pat sits down on his knee, and immediately they set to with some serious snogging. Sue and I look at each other, then look down.

"When the rain comes, they run and hide their heads..."

We've been set up. Sue, I think, must have had some inkling, for she's really made an effort and dressed up, while I, in blissful ignorance, have turned up in dirty jeans and an old jumper with holes in. Sue has washed her hair, which shines lustrously, while mine hangs lank and streaky. She smells alluringly of shampoo and soap and perfume, while I… I don't like to think what I might smell like. But she seems unperturbed and gamely tries to talk above the music.

"You like The Beatles then?" she offers helpfully.

"Yes, I… do," I peter out.

"I prefer The Stones."

"Oh, I like them too."

"Do you want to dance?"

Alarmed, I clutch at the only straw I can think of. "I'd prefer to go for a walk."

"It's raining," she says.

"Yeah, but still… We could always take your umbrella," I say, noticing it bright and red by her handbag.

"OK," she shrugs. "I'll just get my coat."

"Right. Er – Dave, Pat? We're just going out."

They don't even come up for air. Dave merely signals a thumbs-up with his free hand, which Pat then wraps back around her.

Once outside, Sue puts up her umbrella and we start walking along the road. "Where are we going?" she asks, reasonably enough.

"This is your neck of the woods, not mine."

"Oh," I say. I haven't thought this far. Then inspiration hits. "The youth club."

If she feels disappointment, she doesn't show it, and it occurs to me that I unexpectedly have the chance to be really smooth and cool. "Here," I say, "let me carry that." And I take the umbrella in one hand, while in the same movement seamlessly put my other arm around her shoulder. Immediately, and quite thrillingly, Sue places her arm around my waist. I know that I'm instantly blushing. But suddenly it all becomes easier. Conversation begins to flow, she even laughs at one of my jokes, and as the warm spring rain falls softly on our hands and faces, the nervousness drops away.

We approach the pub where it is rumoured they serve anyone – not that I know first hand – but we pass it by. It's not worth the risk of a humiliating refusal in pursuit of the dubious kudos of a pint of shandy and a Cherry B, and as we arrive at Wibbersley Park, at the youth club, I know it's going to be fine. It's a Saturday and so it's only the older teenagers who are there, and because, mercifully, there is no disco on that night, it is fairly quiet. We find a secluded corner to sit, we drink non-alcoholic cider, and we chat – about school, what we hope to do after 'O' levels (in less than a month's time), TV programmes, where we live, our families. It turns out that Sue lives in Astley Road, at number 24, just a couple of doors away from where my grandmother lived when *she* was 16, and here we are, in Wibbersley Park, where she had worked as a nurse during World War 1. I don't share this coincidence with Sue, I keep it to myself, a warm, quiet secret – like being tucked up in a blanket when you're not feeling well. Except that I feel great.

But all too soon the evening comes to a close. At half past nine Sue indicates that we should be heading back. "Mrs Randall will drive me and Pat back to the ferry, and my dad will be there to meet us on the other side. If I'm later than half ten, there'll be hell to pay."

We walk the mile and a half back to Dave's, where he and Pat seem to be locked together in the same clinch as when we left them, and Mrs Randall duly drives us all down Irlam Road to the ferry, retracing the route my grandmother would have taken on her brother's bicycle half a century before. The rain has stopped but a mist is rising from the waters of the canal. The ferry is rowed slowlyacross to where we wait. Dave and Pat are still kissing, while Sue and I have fallen silent. At the last moment she turns towards me and says, "Thanks, Chris. I've had a lovely evening." Then she closes her eyes and lifts up her face towards me. I know I'm expected to kiss her, but suddenly I'm struck down with nervousness once more. I've never kissed anyone before and I'm acutely aware that I'm not really sure what to do. I bend my face towards hers, clumsily, our noses get in each other's way, and my lips brush hers for barely a millisecond, when Mrs Randall calls out, "The ferry's here." Before either of us can say anything else, she is standing aboard with Pat and disappearing into the mist and the darkness. Like Eurydice.

But I am no Orpheus, and as the days and then weeks slip by, and I get caught up in exams, all of a sudden the summer is over and I haven't tried to get in touch with her. I hear from Dave that she has left school and got a good job in an office in Manchester, while I am indeed staying on in the 6th form. She won't want to go out with a schoolboy, I glumly think, and so I never contact her again. Years later I learn that she has become engaged to another boy I was at school with, Carl, who himself lives next door to the girl I will eventually marry, but on that dark and misty Saturday night I don't even know of her existence. Carl and Sue emigrate to Australia, where, for all I know, they still are. But all of that is years ahead. After the ferry has finally slipped completely out of sight, I turn to Dave and Mrs Randall and say, "If you don't mind, I think I'll walk home. It's not far."

And that is what I do. I walk the mile and a half back to Flixton, thinking of Sue heading back to the same road my grandmother had grown up in, and when I finally reach home, she is just making a hot water bottle to take up to bed. My mum and dad are out, probably to the pictures and afterwards a drink.

"Goodnight, Nanna. I hope you didn't wait up for me."

"Oh no. I've had a proper telly night – *Dixon of Dock Green, Morecambe & Wise, Opportunity Knocks*."

"That's alright then. Who won?"

"A lovely Welsh lass – Mary something-or-other… *Those Were The Days*."

"So you've had a nice evening?"

"Yes, love. I have. But not as nice as someone I could mention."

"What do you mean?"

"You look like the cat who got the cream. What's her name?" My grandmother never misses a trick. "But you've not been out like that, have you? Fancy," she continues, looking disapprovingly at my dirty jeans, "going on a date in your overalls!"

"She lives on Astley Road."

"Does she now? That speaks well of her. And where did you take her?"

"The youth club. Wibbersley Park."

"You certainly know how to sweep a girl off her feet, don't you?"

And she tells me again about how Wibbersley Park

had been turned into a military hospital during the first World War, and how she had cycled there as a girl, all the way from Irlam, across the lock gates, over the ferry, and volunteered as a nurse, except this time I properly take it in.

"The things I saw there," she says. "Terrible things. I'd never have imagined that it would see happy times again. I wasn't surprised the Stotts never went back, nor was I sorry when the house was pulled down." She walks towards me and pats me on the shoulder. "Those were the days... Goodnight, Christopher. I'm so pleased." She climbs the stairs, humming Mary Hopkin to herself, thinking of her lost brother.

Later, in bed, I replay the whole evening again and again, like each time I buy a new Beatles record, over and over till I've got it by heart.

Monday's Child has learned to tie his bootlace...
See how they run...

Gwenda Takes Me In Hand

Now you know that you are real
Show your friends that you and me
Belong to the same world
Turned on the same word
Have you heard…?

(The Moody Blues)

"The trouble is you look like a school boy."

"I *am* a schoolboy."

"Not for much longer. You'll be at university in a few weeks. You don't want to turn up looking like this, do you?"

Personally I couldn't see what was wrong with how I looked, but then again I'd never given it much thought either, just grabbed whatever was at hand. This evening I was still in what passed for my school uniform. So was Gwenda. Though I had to admit she looked a lot better in hers than I did in mine. I leant across to kiss her.

"Later," she said. "Homework first. English. I've got a *Hamlet* essay. You?"

"T.S. Eliot."

"*We are the hollow men*," she chanted, "*we are the stuffed men*," dancing round the living room with comical, stiff scarecrow arms, her father's white shirt (which she'd commandeered and customised for school) dangling low over her wrists. She was a complete one-off, with a real flair for design, inherited perhaps from Kathryn, her older sister, a fashion student, who lived wickedly with her boyfriend in a flat in glamorous, bohemian Didsbury.

"We'll take you to Manchester on Saturday and see what we can find for you. You can use your birthday money." (I had just turned 18).

"We?"

"I'll see if Kathryn can come too."

Gwenda's shoulder-length raven hair fell across her pale Vivien Leigh-like face as she bent over her book. I smiled.

"What?"

"*O what a rogue and peasant slave am I…*"

183

"In that case I'd better start cracking my whip," she said. "Work."

We settled in companionable silence to read, make notes, begin our respective essays. After an hour, she stood up and stretched, her long white sleeves slipping below her elbows.

"Cup of tea?" she said.

"Please."

When she came back in from the kitchen, she placed the mugs on the floor and sat down next to me on the sofa. She took hold of my hand and said, "Are you looking forward to it?"

"Being a Drama student?" I said.

She nodded.

"I can't wait."

"Have you decided where you are going yet?"

"I'd like to go to Exeter, but my dad thinks I should stay here, go to Manchester."

"It's not his decision though, is it?"

"He has to sign the acceptance form, don't forget."

"But that's ridiculous. They're lowering the age of consent to 18, aren't they?"

"Not till next year. So you'll be OK. Technically, I'll not be an adult till I'm 21."

"It wouldn't apply to me in any case. My parents would support me wherever I chose."

I shrugged.

"It'll work out," she said. "He'll come round. Let *me* talk to him. I'll charm him."

"Right," I said, smiling. "My mum and dad don't really approve of you."

("You've changed since you met that Gwenda," they'd said.

"Good," I'd replied).

"Well, *I* don't approve of *them*."

*

184

The next Saturday we took the number 5 bus to Manchester where we met Kathryn at *The Kardomah*, already sipping an espresso and smoking a black sobranie. (I'd only just experienced my first Maxwell House).

"Well," she said, "we can start on New Brown Street if you like. *Stolen from Ivor* have just opened their first out of London store there – what do you say to a Ben Sherman shirt, Chris? – but personally I'd head for the second hand market stalls in The Corn Exchange and the textile warehouses on Ancoats Street. What do you think, Chris?"

The two sisters looked at me expectantly.

"Do I have a choice?" I said.

"Honestly," said Gwenda, "he's hopeless." And off they went, arms linked, with me trailing in their wake.

"Right," said Kathryn, as we reached the first shop. "Ready for the fray?"

"As ready as I'll ever be," I said.

"You don't really need me, do you, Gwenda? I promised to meet up with Barry at eleven. We'll see you in Tommy Duck's in a couple of hours, and we'll take stock, shall we? Have fun, Chris," and with a wink she was gone.

"Come on," said Gwenda, looking at my less than enthusiastic expression. "It's not like going to the dentist's." Just at that moment, going to the dentist's seemed a much more preferable option.

She took my hand and for the next couple of hours or so we traipsed from shop to shop, with me trying on item after item that she picked out for me.

"I've only got £15," I said.

"It'll be enough. Trust me."

And so it proved. Come the end of the day, I discovered I was the surprised owner of a pair of bottle green cord flares, a button-down paisley shirt, an orange skinny-rib jumper, a pair of brown shoes with a gold buckle instead of laces, with still enough change for a string of turquoise beads Gwenda insisted were needed to complete the outfit. I was dubious about the beads but Kathryn turned up at that point with Barry, her boyfriend, who gave me the once-over and an encouraging thumbs-up.

"All we need now," said Gwenda, "is to do something

with his hair."

Barry, seeing the look on my face, laughed. "Just go with it, mate. Come back to our place and we'll have a beer. It'll help to lessen the pain."

For someone who'd only recently been into a pub to order an under-age shandy, this was heady stuff indeed.

*

Catching the bus home in the evening, Gwenda said, "I don't feel like staying in tonight. Let's go for a drink. I'll just stop off and get changed first, alright?"

While I waited for Gwenda to get ready, I was paraded in front of her mum, who immediately expressed her approval. Mrs Hughes (or Denise, as I was daringly encouraged to call her) was always so easy-going. "Cigarette?" she said.

"Thanks," I said nonchalantly, trying not to let it look like this was the first time a grown-up had offered me one.

Gwenda came down a few minutes later wearing her grandmother's white wedding dress with heavy black eye make-up, black lipstick, and ankle-length black stiletto boots. My jaw hit the floor while Denise burst into applause. "Have fun," she said. "Go knock 'em dead, though I'm not sure that Flixton's ready for the two of you!"

As we walked the half mile to the pub Gwenda had picked out for us to make our appearance, cars hooted their horns, cyclists nearly fell off their bikes and passers-by gaped open-mouthed.

"See," she said. "You're causing a stir already."

I laughed. "I don't think it's me they're staring at."

The old *Union Inn*, at the bottom of Bent Lanes by the overgrown stream known locally as the Bent Brook, which dribbled its way very slowly to the Mersey, had recently changed hands, been refurbished and had just re-opened. (How did Gwenda always seem to know these things?) Renamed *The Fox and Hounds*, its décor was now all hunting brasses and Toby jugs. It was still reasonably early and the pub was quiet, but (unbelievably since this was not his usual watering hole) standing at the bar was my father.

He was with one of his friends from the local Operatic

– Peter, whom I knew by sight, but who didn't know me. As we walked in, Peter put down his pint glass, turned to my father and said in a voice of utter disgust, "My God, look what the wind just blew in."

My father, embarrassed and appalled, pretended not to know me. "Kids today, eh?" he said, turning away.

"They should bring back National Service, that's what I think," said Peter.

"Let's go," I said immediately, completely mortified.

"No way," said Gwenda. "We've as much right to be here as they have." She was enjoying herself hugely. "I'll have a glass of red please."

I went to a different bar to order the drinks, so as not to have to face my father again and cause yet more embarrassment. When I returned to where Gwenda was sitting, I was still seething inside.

"Cheers," she said.

"He'll never sign that acceptance form now."

Gently she placed her hand on my arm. "Give him time to get used to the idea."

I could barely contain myself. "He refused to even acknowledge me."

"He doesn't know who you are."

*

A week later I wore the new clothes for a second time. My hair, in its somewhat alarming Afro, had settled down a bit, and I no longer got a shock each time I caught sight of my reflection.

"I suppose this was that Gwenda's idea," was the only comment my mother could muster. "I expect she thinks it makes you look with it."

And now I was back on the number 5 bus again, heading off to Manchester once more, but alone this time, going to meet up with a couple of mates to see The Moody Blues playing live at The Odeon. Gwenda wasn't coming.

"Why would I?" she'd said when I asked her if she wanted to. "They're rubbish."

I couldn't argue with this. When I'd bought their most

recent LP (*To Our Children's Children's Children*), her derision knew no bounds. "I can't believe it," she said, after the opening poem. "Did he really say what I thought he did? '*With the force of 10 billion butterfly sneezes…*'? Pur-lease!"

Despite their penchant for pretentious poems, declaimed against a background of gongs, roaring winds, electronic bleeps, their overblown, half-baked concepts and their appalling record covers, I retained a huge affection for them, ever since I'd heard their first album a few years back, and I'd kind of grown up with them. *Tuesday Afternoon, Nights in White Satin, Visions of Paradise, Melancholy Man,* they had all somehow reflected the zeitgeist for me. (I never was at what you might call the cutting edge. No Captain Beefheart for me sadly).

Ah well, as the Moody Blues' song *Another Morning* so profoundly puts it, "yesterday's dreams are tomorrow's sighs…!"

I arrived at *The Odeon* just as Robin and Jonnie, my long-term fellow fans, did too. As I crossed the road to join them, they could hardly contain their laughter. "What *do* you look like?" said Robin.

"What d'you mean?"

"Your hair for a start," mocked Jonnie. "You look like you've been dragged through a hedge backwards."

"That's good then, isn't it?" I said.

"And those shoes?" pointed Robin, grimacing. "You look ridiculous. Like a highwayman."

I rather liked the idea of that. "Stand and deliver!" I said. "Have you got the tickets?"

We went in and the concert was much like previous ones I'd attended. Jonnie and Robin were full of it afterwards. "Fantastic," they enthused.

"I never thought they'd play *Legend of a Mind* live," said Jonnie, and he and Robin immediately began to sing. "*He'll take you up, he'll take you down, he'll plant your feet back on the ground….*"

Gwenda's right, I thought. This really is rubbish. I'll be at university in a few weeks, while Jonnie and Robin are still just schoolboys. I could feel myself leaving an old life behind.

Jonnie had the new record he'd just bought from the

merchandise desk after the concert tucked under his coat to protect it from the rain that was now beginning to fall. "Want to come round tomorrow to listen to it?" he said.

"Absolutely," said Robin. "Chris?"

"I don't think I can, mate. I think Gwenda and I have got something planned."

"Suit yourself," said Jonnie.

Just then the bus came up, driving straight through a deep puddle soaking my new cords and shoes.

"Shit," I yelled, while they just pissed themselves laughing.

"Serves you right," they said.

Two months later Gwenda dumped me. The next day I started listening to Leonard Cohen.

Penny Bridge

"The greawnd it sturr'd beneath my feet…"
Samuel Bamford: *Tim Bobbin's Grave*

I'm back in the town I was a teenager in. Shaw Town. Though it's not called that now. Nor was it then. That belongs to an older time, two and a half centuries ago, when it was merely a collection of outlying farms spread along the water meadows on the flood plains between the Mersey and the Irwell.

John Collier lived there, a lace maker (like my great grandmother), who took from his trade the name he is better known by: Tim Bobbin, the father of Lancashire dialect writing. His most enduring work, *Human Passions Delineated, or Tummus & Mary*, tells a simple love story between a dairyman and a milkmaid.

Hard to credit when I was approaching 18 with the steel works across the canal, the heavy visible industry of Trafford Park just three miles away (where my father worked in an asbestos factory), and the huge petro-chemical works at Partington closer still. A permanent eerie glow hung above them every night as the sky burned red like Mordor.

But there were still traces of the old Shaw Town to be found if you knew where to look, where Tummus might have wooed his Mary: the Cinder Track that ran from Acre Gate to Abbotsfield over Penny Bridge by way of the railway line and the Thunder Tunnel, a low arch directly under the track where, as small children, we'd crouch waiting for a train to thunder over us shrieking at the tops of our voices, or later a trysting place for courting couples; then up through The Grove to the Jubilee Tree and the Village Green.

Such anomalies, these names – Acre Gate a demolished farm; Abbotsfield an overgrown waste ground where wild dogs roamed; The Grove a rat-infested slum, and the Village Green only an old road sign by a pub car park. Hardly known then; resurrected now by property developers as misleading names for new estates.

The Cinder Track remains however, still unadopted, still unsurfaced, and Penny Bridge still crosses the railway. You can still follow this path on old maps threading its way across fields, between farms, all the way to Barton Dock, linking the Irwell to the Mersey over several miles, and, a few weeks after my 18th birthday, I walked its entire length, trying to reclaim a sense of continuity, some kind of timeline, weaving between more recent marks on the land.

From Brooklyn Grange to De Brook Court Farm
The road runs ever on
Copper beech tree, sycamore
Lean towards the sun
And grow….

I suppose I fancied myself as Tummus, always looking for my Mary – not that I'd have admitted this to anyone. I'd have got pretty short shrift if I had.

Now, four and more decades later, I retrace my steps. I lean on the granite stone wall of Penny Bridge looking out across the water meadows, those few patches of green still not built on, down towards the thirties estate I lived on back then, close to Stott's Orchard, gone now. It's early. A mist rises from the river, creeping towards me along the track. I see my younger self emerging from it, striding confidently towards me, his arm around a pretty girl with raven black hair. They are both talking animatedly as they head down towards the Thunder Tunnel, a few yards below me. They disappear from view but snatches of what they are saying drift up to me. They are arguing about the future…

"I'm thinking of staying," I hear myself say. "I've got a place at Manchester. I can go there."
"And live at home?"
"No. I'll get a bed-sit."
"Where?"
"Moss Side. I've already looked. It's just across the road from the Student Union."
"But you'll not get a grant. You'll have to go back home."
"I'd manage."

191

"The whole point of university is to get away, find out who you really are."

"But I feel I belong here." I'm struggling now. "This place, this track, these fields. I feel connected." I'm looking straight at her.

"Oh no," she says. "That's way too much responsibility. You can't stay here because of me. This time next year it'll be my turn to make this choice, and I'm telling you right now, there's no way I'm staying here. I'm leaving and I'm not coming back. You won't see me for dust…"

And I see her now in my mind's eye storming out across the fields back towards the main road. A train roars across the Thunder Tunnel drowning out my shouts of pain and anguish, but after it's gone, it just becomes mixed with the raucous racket of rooks, the low rumble of distant traffic, just distant background noise, a constant buzzing tinnitus that never quite goes away.

Years later I finally left this Mersey flood plain, crossed the city to an old cotton town just to the north. I only discovered when we got there that this is the path Tim Bobbin had also taken. In a Rochdale churchyard an unremarkable head stone marks his grave, on which is inscribed the epitaph he himself wrote, just twenty minutes before he died:

Jack of all trades – left to lie i' th' dark…

Time to let in the light.

Circuit Training

my girlfriend's in serious training
for next month's north of England championships
which means early to bed and early to rise
no alcohol, no chocolate, no sex
only endless circuits, round and round

in readiness for the big race
the four hundred metres
one final circuit, a single lap
taken at full speed till completely spent
the final dip before she breasts the tape

high on fumes of embrocation
I didn't make it past the warm up track
consigned to back-straight backwaters
carrying the kit, holding the thermos
behind-hand butt of backseat jokes

but still I persevered, kept the faith
wore the T-shirt, waved the rattle
shouting her name from the back of the stands
snapping her photo on top of the podium
she won my heart, I lost the race

A Folk Play

(Isle of Man 1973)

I am listening to the wind
rattling the chains in the harbour
restless it will not release me
gusting my thoughts round and round
meanwhile – in the next room
my girlfriend sleeps with her sister

I am walking the cliffs in the morning
I am pointing out landmarks of interest
the lighthouse, the Chasms, the circles of stone
my girlfriend and her sister
keep their counsel close

I am studying the past
the island's folk traditions
the beginnings of drama in seasonal rituals
hunting the wren, the boat supper
I am writing my thesis
the rain is rapping the window
the mist is thickening
I am asking a series of questions
she is looking out to sea
the clock is ticking between us
in the rented fisherman's cottage

we are strangers
at the ceilidh we learn a courting dance
the locals are watching us
our fingers form the shape of lougtan sheep
our horns interlock, she curtseys
my leg passes over her head
our limbs entwine by the fire
our bodies blur in the glimmer

I am entering her flesh
I am becoming somebody else
I am becoming her
I am whispering I love her
she is shivering in a corner
I am not your mirror, she is shouting
her tears on my cheeks are like razors
I will not be one of your ghosts

I am catching a bus
I am crossing the island
from east to west, and south to north
it is a journey which takes me all day
I have appointments in Ballasalla
where the last person alive
who speaks no English will see me
I am standing on the threshold
the rain slants in from the sea
nobody answers my calling
curtains are closed to the day
I am listening at the keyhole
a woman is rhythmically sobbing
to the drip of a broken tap

a candle is guttering, broken
I watch it fade at the window
it welcomes the traveller's return
but the chair by the fire is empty
it rocks by itself in the silence
the ashes lie cold on the hearth
on the mantelpiece is a letter
she is gone with her sister to England
she writes that she is dead
she can no longer speak my language
she died before I could see her
you are studying the past, she tells me
these are my ashes study me

alone in the fisherman's cottage
I am writing my thesis
I have my camera, my tape-recorder
my box-file of newspaper cuttings
I am sifting for traces that linger
invoking the souls of the dead
I am recording their absence on paper
myths and superstitions
a forgotten folk memory

I am pacing the cottage at night
I see her face in the mirror
I hear her tread on the stair
she washes her hair in the kitchen
she sings her sister to sleep
she is wrong
she is a ghost already
her imprint's stamped on my skin

children in rags and feathers
knock on my door after sunset
they are singing the *hop tu naa*
they are calling the harvest home
farmers tie crosses of mountain ash
to the tails of fattened cattle
with hanks of green wool they drive them
through fires of blackened stubble

I am watching men weaving women
maidens from last year's corn
they are breaking their bodies and singing
they burn on the bonfires like witches
huge on the towering stooks
the children are carrying dead birds
slung between riven poles
they are roasting the hearts on a spit
and eating them with relish

I am building a shrine
her photograph burns on the grate
I remember her tearing my letters
I remember her cutting her hair
I remember her sloughing me from her
these are my ashes study me

we are acting out our own folk play
repeating the doggerel rhymes
who is St George? who the dragon?
who is the Betsy, the Fool?
the poetry is the Doctor
giving back life to the dead

I am studying the past
I am casting out nets in the darkness
I am trawling for stories
I am diving for treasure
instead I find only shipwrecks

I am standing on the deck of a ship
I am leaving the island
the mist magically clears
Manannan is mocking me
I am closing the book
I am writing the last full stop
a sense of relief that it's over

my thesis lies in the museum
covered in dust, unread

Skinny-Dipping in the Med

(Le Vieux-Nice 1971)

high on cheap wine and cannabis
thirty British students touring France
in a beat-up red London bus
taking the Scottish play across Provence
hang out all night on a beach near Nice

I play many parts - the Doctor
witnessing the sleepwalking scene,
half of Birnam Wood, a Murderer,
reporting portents as an Old Man
and, this night, the Drunken Porter

singing, badly, Leonard Cohen
while others frolic and cavort -
I strum along impressing no one,
the girl I fancy's making out
with the guy who's playing Duncan

and I want to travel with her
and I want to travel blind
while the sound of lust and laughter
surges with the tide across the sand
and the camp fire flames rise higher

All Right Now and *I Feel Free*
the party ratchets up a gear
we're on our feet and dancing wildly
it's what we've *come together* for
and *where we're meant to be*

and all as one we race into the sea
howling the moon, tearing off clothes

our new shiny bodies slippery
eels diving through and over waves
and suddenly she's next to me

the water round her rages, boils
she rises like a mermaid from below
we try on this new skin, these scales
her tail's ferocious undertow –
but I can't follow where she calls...

washed up like seals basking in the sand
the sea now just a hush, a whisper
more smokes and joints are passed around
After the Gold Rush, Helter Skelter
tomorrow and tomorrow and –

although I won't remember what we said
or did or any of those other things
WE WENT SKINNY-DIPPING IN THE MED(!!)
and what next year, next day, next minute brings
who *gives* a shit – we might be dead!

Snake in the Grass

(Sevagram, Maharashtra, Central India)

a night snake secretly unseen
slides down towards me from the eaves
to where we sit sipping spiced tea
on the makeshift verandah

silently, inexorably
it seeks me out, its slow moves
patient, stealthy and sure
till, ready, it rears its head to strike –

with barely a backward glance
she plucks it from behind my ear
hurls it in a high wide arc
through the bougainvillea leaves...

this morning, she tells me, she woke
with one coiled close beside her
on the pillow peacefully
winding out and through between

the knotted rope and crack
of fevered truckle dreams
tomorrow it will shed its skin
which she'll nail to a boundary fence –

a warning, don't come near –
a trophy to discarded loves...

later her father takes me back
I ride pillion on his scooter
head thrown back, a rictus grin
racing past abandoned farms

beneath a hunter's moon
we tear through unmarked field graves
where snakes new hatched writhe in wait for me –
they've been waiting ever since...

Pebble

(La Ciotat, near Marseille)

words roll round your tongue
unfamiliar and strange
pebble swelling against palate
roof, speech and thought

slurring, each tiny droplet
in fierce Midi heat
you suck evaporates
each dry consonant, grates

no English, she says –
no French, no kisses –
bikini top unhooks
attise érotique

slides slow and down
stopping at shoreline
she turns, waves, walks
into the sea, sucks

the sand beneath your feet,
undertow heart beat,
urging you to come
deeper where water's warm

salt speckling skin and lips…
your first few tentative steps
stutter at water's edge
from where, rooted, you watch

her swim away, each stroke
sure and confident takes
her from you further –
you do not try to stop her

no words, just thoughts
half formed stick in your throat
each disgorging reflex
gags, convulses, chokes

expels the pebble whole
smooth and worn with all
those unsaid words, those unlived lives
spits it, skating on the waves

on and on you watch it skim
towards the far horizon's rim
caught by the sun's green ray
le rayon vert qui s'est fané…

treading water, the long wait
her hand shoots up to pluck it
from the air, place it deep inside
her skin to catch the next tide

a life imagined, a moment lost…
clouds mass in the east
you pull on your coat, turn
back to more known terrain

A Day in the Life

(Edinburgh)

she pushes her tongue in my ear
she tells me she's from Texas
she's taking time out she says
will I be her study buddy…?

she's teaching me to drive
putting me through her paces
jumping me through her hoops
you jive pretty good white boy

shift she says when she means change gear
hang a right when she wants me to turn
we're learning a whole new language
I'd love to turn you on

step on the gas under the hood
hey baby you stick pretty good
hitching a ride, taking a trip
a new kind of special relationship…

*

I'm lying on the top floor of an Edinburgh tenement
a crack of light in the granite sky
the night air riffles the threadbare curtain
strung on a makeshift cord across the skylight
the noise of traffic below, the snores and snuffles
of stoned and wasted students flat-out on the floor

just as I'm drifting off I hear a noise
a muffled tapping on the broken pane
a dustbin lid clattering down a back alley
a startled fox, a stroppy gull, the tinkling of glass
and a whispered "shit", then the light foot-fall of
someone landing softly, like a cat -

she came in through the bathroom window –
"Sorry, hope I didn't wake anyone?"
she hadn't, we were all of us anyway far too gone –
except for me… I'm on red alert

she looks around the room
at the bodies sprawled in sleeping bags
like sacks of coal tipped on the floor
she lets her eyes accustom
then picks her way between them
like a ballet dancer on pointe

she tilts her head to one side
scrutinising each shape as an alien might
for evidence of life, for signs of recognition
until she reaches me, I hold my breath
I shut my eyes, feigning sleep
she leans in closer, pauses, sniffs

satisfied she straightens up, breathes
and in one swift decisive movement
peels off her dress and climbs
luxuriously into my sleeping bag
where now there are definite signs of life
and sleep can no longer be feigned…

she said she'd always been a dancer
she worked at fifteen clubs a day
and though she thought I knew the answer
well I knew but I could not say

uh-oh…
she stops…
oops, sorry -
wrong guy

and with the same easy American nonchalance
as when she thought she'd found me she slips out
steps between the sleeping bodies
in search of the right stuff

wrong guy
the wrong man
the odd man out

the goodbye girl
looking for mister goodbar
the spy who came in from the cold

hello goodbye

First Night Nerves

we are sitting on the sofa
the overture has ended
the needle sticks on the record
a pause
worthy of a Pinter play
hangs in the hiss of the gas fire
we stare into it waiting for
that small inner voice to say
beginners please
but we've not yet explored
the whole script, stage fright's descended
on us, rehearsal time's over

we don't know if tonight will
run strictly according to plot
neither of us speaks the minutes
tick by
our eyes are mirrors where we check
appearances one last time
before the house lights start to dim
is it too late to back
out, fight shy
of hurried mistimed exits
to the bedroom before we get
our cue, this is our final call

The Horse In The Yard

Each morning, as the Liverpool to Manchester
train rattled across the iron bridge, I looked
for her between the caged mesh of girder
and sky. Below, where the last derelict
railway arches stamped across the wrecked
wasteland, and the brown scum of the canal sucked
the life out of the city, I sought her;

and there, beneath the penultimate arch,
in a bricked-up builder's yard, I'd catch
a glimpse of her, golden in the grey grime,
sunlight glistening on her flanks, a flame
of chestnut in the morning monochrome.
She'd throw back her head in a silent scream
of shunting engines, clanking chains, the screech
of brakes, and the train, like my heart, would lurch

as it clattered into Knott Mill Station
to face the fumes, the noise, the dirt, the dust;
but above the sounds of demolition
I heard that whinny of exaltation
pierce the pavements cracking in the frost,
shatter stained glass windows in the disused
warehouses, not knowing till I missed
her once, that to see her had become
nothing less than a compulsion.

It was as the homeward train re-crossed
the city, back towards the iron bridge,
framed against bars of rain and steel, I first
saw you, skittering across the carriage,
chestnut hair cascading as you tossed
your head, your eyes met mine, a wounded beast,
cautious, cornered. A falling chimney thrust
its silhouette against the water's edge
in a final, broken, jagged fist;
and as the walls came down I felt a pledge
fulfilled: we stepped out from an unlocked cage.

Only in Brighton

Sauron the Dark Lord
playing Frisbee with his pals
on a Brighton beach

launches a high wide
perfect parabola, one
ring to rule them all

Gaudete

*Gaudete - an anonymous plainsong from the early 15th century collection Priori
Cantones made famous by Steeleye Span in the 1970's. (See end for translations)*

Heard in Blackpool 1975, remembered now – for Gareth: 1953 – 2013

the day passes in a blur
a loop of light around your head
kicking a football on a beach
crystals of sand in your hair
a Frisbee frozen in mid
flight which when I try to catch

it down the years, to grasp
it, hold it close, eludes
me, flutters down, a dip and curve
back to each memory's cusp
flickering with your eyelid's
pulse, the seagulls' wild dive

swooping as we race the waves
and though you cannot swim
you smile as we go under –
all the sounds of muffled lives
crashing like an unheard drum
rise up through the half glimpsed future

jolting me awake, that same song's
call to arms now turned to lament
carmina laetitiae
devote redamus flings
a faint rebuke defiant
undiminished since the day

we first heard it soar above
the crowd and out across the town
back towards the water's edge
your footprints in the sand leave
no trace along the shore line
as from the haze you re-emerge

striding with that Ghost Train grin
fearless through each fairground
ride, haunted swing, hall of mirrors
where each phantom broken
image carries no cruel hand
print yet of what mockeries

lie in wait, the Golden Mile
kiss-me-quick/squeeze-me-slow
souvenirs, like candy floss,
which innocently beguile…
tempus ad est gratiae
hoc quod optabamus

I try to fix that summer blur
now, capture in a single frame
that one-time shot to take me back
to that always golden hour
your whoop of joy urging home
the Frisbee's final hanging arc

Translations from the Latin:
Gaudete   Rejoice
Carmina laetitiae devote redamus   *We offer these songs of joy with love*
                                                         afflicted

Tempus ad est gratiae hoc quod   *Let us give thanks for this time of*
optabamus   *grace - we long for its return*

6

Graduation

What Survives

But if you place each rescued moment of high alert
beneath the latest high-spec microscope
to probe beyond the loss and the regret
and salvage what survives of each first spark of hope

what will I do if, when you load the slide
with this or that culture on the tray,
adjust the focus, magnify the lens,
you tell me what survives has drained away;

how am I then to see what happens
washed up with the rubbish on the tide:
do I sieve the filtered water pure
or drink untreated sewage raw?

No – rather I'll explore fresher, less primeval slime;
hold my breath, dive deeper to a half-remembered home...

Not Fade Away

(Inspired by a screening of the 1957 Universal film of Jack Arnold's 'The Incredible Shrinking Man' based on the Richard Matheson novel)

sixty years ago since last you saw me
size of a hat pin wrestling spiders –
I survived

banished to this basement bunker
cellar steps as Himalayan peaks
I endured

hat pin now a Dubai skyscraper
ventilator grille whose bars
I slip between

no longer a prison holding me
cut loose from gravity untethered
I'm escaping

floating like thistledown
radiation cloud half life
I'm returning to

mingling with motes of sunlight
caught and glistening each morning
I'm drifting

hung in the hush of star fall
the twilight zone, the outer limits
I'm becoming

sub-atomic particle floating through time
no matter how small I shrink
I matter

Alter Egos

You could always depend on Tonto,
the trusty right hand,
the ever present friend,
faithful Indian companion, who

heard the far off warning sound
of no-good 'ornery outlaws
or the thundering iron horse
just by laying his ear to the ground,

always kept to the straight and narrow,
reliably saved the worst of days
with a wise, well chosen phrase
and a carefully aimed arrow:

even good man must wear mask
some time, kemo sabe,
white man natural state not happy –
we rode disguised into the dusk…

*

When Gary Sobers strolled to the crease,
bat swinging casually,
collar turned up nonchalantly,
acknowledging the applause,

you knew the sun was sure to shine,
crowds dancing in the stands,
calypso cricket, steel bands,
an endless flow of rum and wine.

I was more in the Barrington mould –
the safety-first art
of implacable dead bat,
extra sweater to keep out the cold.

How I longed to be like Gary,
cast caution to the wind,
throw back my head and sing
even as skies turned gloomy,

so when those storm clouds finally massed
I heard that golden rising song
in cadenced Caribbean twang:
summer's like Sobers, too good to last...

*

Punch was a most unusual ally –
holy fool,
lord of misrule,
wicked gleam in his eye –

he wormed his way to my darkest dream
on a pier in North Wales
thrilling me with lurid tales
of revolution, murder, mayhem,

cast off cosy domesticity,
cheated the hangman, tricked the police,
hoodwinked the devil to gain his release,
always courting my complicity

which I gave him, threw in my lot
with him for a while,
adopted his stick, his swazzle, his smile,
thought: that's the way to do it...

*

Unlike many other kids I knew
I didn't have imaginary friends
who'd take the blame or make amends
or be there simply to talk to

until uninvited Camille stepped out
of the dansette in the sitting room

(exotic sounding *nom de plume*
through whom I'd place each daily bet)

straight from Lehar's light opera,
my father's high tenor voice
transporting me to a place
gilded with glamour…

*

But with none of these travel companions
was I able to stay the course.
I watched each one saddle his horse,
leave me behind with my diffidence.

Camille stayed longer than most –
perhaps because he wasn't real
he was someone I could feel
closer to than the rest

but he too left eventually
so it came as quite a shock
when out of the blue he came back –
I thought I'd forgotten him completely –

in Graham Nash's northern tones
oh Camille, tell me how do you feel
now your heart tells you this can't be real
bringing with him all those former friends

who whisper in my ear slyly,
who hit me for six,
beat me with their sticks –
time to tell truth now, kemo sabe…

Ghosts

we see ourselves everywhere
ghosts walking across the city
hands raised in recognition
rediscovered turns of phrase
welcoming us back

First Day

This first day
sitting in regimented rows
we wait for people to arrive
for things to begin.

Some have already broken the ice –
halting laughter mixes with the scrape of chairs on vinyl
as ranks break, then reform
into nervous conversation groups.
Not me though –
I watch from the sidelines
feeling suddenly very young.

What am I doing here?
How will I fit in
with all these mature

                confident

                        cultured accents?
The young man next to me reaches across
holds out his hand formally for me to shake
announces his surname and the public school he's from.

Moments later the Professor arrives –
the room quietens,
heads turn towards him
expectant.
He describes the syllabus
(names I haven't heard of)
and I'm even more convinced
I'm in the wrong room

              there must be some mistake

                  I didn't get a place here after all.

Around noon
dismissed for the day
I find myself walking down the City Road –
the local boy sharing the sights

the cabbie displaying the knowledge
the trader shouting his wares
desperate to impress.

This is the theatre
               there's the cathedral
                           here's the oldest
pub in the city –
The Shambles
 (before the IRA bombed the Arndale
before there even was an Arndale).

We stumble through the demolition
                     the building sites
                            the cranes
our own unimagined futures forming in the dust and ruins
sprawling scaffold towers blocking out the sun
reinventing phoenix-like the city we climb up out of
the wreckage of past lives shed like snakeskin
glimpsing the ghosts of who we might become
waiting there to greet us in hard hats.

Beside me walks a future CEO
                  heroin addict
                        politician
                              playwright
and a girl who'll read the news.

The hard hats reach across the rubble smiling
before they haul us back up to the light.

Alma Mater

("Easy to open, push hard": sign on a door)

Back on the campus
of my old *alma mater,*
seeking the familiar
among the sleek glass

towers sprung up since,
I spot the old German
church still hunkered down
beside the picket fence

where I studied Drama...
Forty years have passed since then
that set the wheels in motion
to all that's led to this summer's

pilgrimage to return here
hoping to find... what exactly?
The truth of it eludes me –
when just as I reach the door

("easy to open, push hard")
a flock of Asian girls
surges past me, high-pitched squeals
like the song of some exotic bird

uncaged, set free to scatter
as confetti on the wind;
they flutter to the ground
followed a few moments later

by an older student, hair
framing her face, head down
mumbling sorry, *aisumesen,*
mind completely elsewhere,

drawing a cigarette
half way to her mouth, she wears
what might be an old U.S.
Marine combat jacket

looking for all the world
through the rimless tinted lenses
of my John Lennon glasses
like Yoko Ono, she holds

the door open for me –
echoes of student protest
roar up from the past
and briefly it is 1970

once more, till she takes out
her cell, flips it open, checks
for updates, missed calls, texts
and the door slams shut.

The mirage fades and here am I,
an old guy in his 60's,
hair unfashionably long, whose
parade has passed him by.

I check my own phone –
a message tells me I've been
tagged, sender's name withheld, I turn
and there I am at 21:

this younger version of me
seems to sense my shadow
falling briefly in the glow
of that endless hazy

campus afternoon,
he sits up shielding his eyes
which seem to recognise
me, masked by the sun,

and beckons me across.
I shake my head – that was then –

he smiles, lies back down again
as if to say, could be worse,

stretched out easy on the grass
carefree, golden, finals over,
his eyes scan a future
whose promises seem endless...

The Japanese girl appears
invisible at his side –
see, he says, life's not so bad –
a tear catches me unawares...

Rain suddenly rips
the sky, we run helter skelter
seeking refuge, shelter
beneath bending tree tops

where the Asian girls alight,
shiver like dancing leaves,
the frisson of old loves
shimmering out of sight,

leaving a faint trace,
a pale palimpsest
of lingered lives lost
unflattening the grass.

I head back toward
the door of the German church,
I lift its creaking latch –
easy to open, push hard...

Strawberry Mark

they're pulling down the seventies
halls of residence tower block
I remember first being built
when I was a student here...

over four years I watched it grow
mushroom the sky, blot out the sun
shrug off its concrete pupa
unshackled from scaffold chains

unpinned hawk moth carapace
folded wings of plated glass
transporting me to higher realms
above congested underpasses

ascending from these lower depths
I'd ride up on the escalator
convinced of someone following,
shadow on the stair, whisper in my ear

I'd turn around – no one
(Eurydice fading)
to the book shop on its first floor mall
along with discount travel agents

exotic fruit and flower stalls
lure of far away places
poster destinations gliding
either side the moving walkway...

now this skeletal hulk
stands silhouetted
as birds and clouds sail through
its roofless windowless edifice

outlines of one or two
single rooms remain intact

scraps of posters flapping
torn and charred memories

marches and sit-ins
endless earnest debates
Mao and Ché and Joni Mitchell
benignly smiling down

there was a girl I used to visit here
her room high up on the seventh floor
looked out across the city
street lights burning beneath invisible stars

that empty shell above me
concrete posts like jagged fists
protests wilting in the rain
might have been the exact spot

where once I kissed her
she had a strawberry mark
that bloomed on her cheek when she smiled
I haven't thought of her in years

the demolition wrecking ball
swings and smashes through
the last remaining bones
come crashing to the ground

scatter as cement dust clears
sunset spreads like spilt paint
streaks the chrysalis sky with red
a slow suffusing strawberry mark

light tapping on my shoulder...

Printer's Devil*

past The Printer's Devil
boarded up abandoned pub
time taps me on the shoulder
fetches ink and setting type
to help me write this down

granddad's print works
where mum would dance as a girl
to rolling presses' rhythm
where I learned to read
wooden blocks with fingers
now boarded up too

*[*a printer's devil was an apprentice in a printer's establishment who performed a
number of tasks, such as mixing tubs of ink and fetching type]*

Frozen Glove

large glove lies frozen in the lane
fingers outstretched, stiff to my touch
years now since my son's curled fist
sought my waiting hand

I walk again past the glove, stone cold, unpicked
I'm reminded now of granddad
in whose hands hammer, saw or plane
were a perfect fit

by contrast my own hands are empty
not even holding a pen
instead fingers tap on laptop
beside silent book-lined walls

Delivering Memories

If ever I'm asked what has been my favourite job, I answer immediately: driving a delivery van for a local florist's, for the simple reason that everyone was always so pleased to see me. Except for once. I arrived on the doorstep of a thirties semi early one morning bearing a beautiful, wrapped bouquet of mixed blooms, to be greeted by a young woman still in her dressing gown. She took one look at the flowers and was instantly horrified: "You can't deliver those," she said. "My husband is here!" She was just about to shut the door when she added, sotto voce, with a nervous glance over her shoulder, "Come back in half an hour. He'll be gone by then."

Otherwise people were delighted. Even when it was a funeral, they were quietly relieved to see that everything was being done properly. Weddings and funerals were our biggest and most regular orders. Each morning Mr Monks, the owner of the shop, would drive to Smithfield Market in the centre of Manchester before dawn to make sure he had the pick of the freshest flowers as they arrived from the growers. You never quite knew what you were going to get – in February and March it would be daffodils and narcissi from the Isles of Scilly – but he would frequently surprise the rest of us working for him with an unexpected glut of anemones, or dahlias, or freesias. As well as Mr Monks, there was Linda, the shop girl, straight from school, who served the customers; Rosie, the actual florist – "what else could I do with a name like mine?" – who designed and arranged all the displays and who'd been to college; Old Fred, who'd previously driven the van, but who now swept out the cellar, brought more stock up when it was needed, and helped out in a whole range of things; and then there was me – just graduated from university, trying to run a small touring theatre company with friends, working for a drinking buddie of my dad's as the delivery boy.

It suited me perfectly, I'd begin work each morning around 7am, deliver flowers till midday, then rehearse all afternoon and evening. As well as the weddings and funerals, we had our weekly round of regular customers: board rooms, hotel foyers, the Mayor's Parlour, council offices, and every

Monday at Kellogg's in Trafford Park, where there were cheerful displays in the two works canteens. I used to enjoy these weekly Kellogg's drop-offs, partly because of the excellent bacon barm cakes they used to serve, but mostly because the previous summer I had worked for a month there, and if delivering flowers was the best job I ever had, working at Kellogg's was up there with the worst. I was what was ludicrously called a "Quality Assurance Operative", which involved me wearing a white lab coat and standing next to a conveyor belt for hours at a time while thousands upon thousands of Corn Flakes flowed past me: if I saw a burnt black one, my job was to lean over and pick it out.

But mostly the work was delivering bouquets to individual houses – wedding anniversaries, birthdays, get well wishes, apologies. Each morning I'd wash the van, clear out all the bits of leaves from the previous day, then load her up with the first set of orders. We delivered to an approximate ten mile radius of the shop, and during my first week, Old Fred would hand me the A to Z and test me on all the roads and pretty soon I got to know them, including all the short cuts, cul de sacs and one way systems. Saturdays were always the busiest days because of the weddings, and I would pick up lots of tips then, too. I would usually be tipped at funerals as well, but more quietly, almost secretively, as a thank you for being discreet and on time. I usually gave these back to whatever charity was being collected for at the service.

This carried on for about six months, by which time I felt like an old hand. More and more Mr Monks would take me with him to Smithfield Market to help him buy from the growers, and once or twice he'd let me go by myself. This meant getting there for 4am, but it was worth it for the overtime, and also for the atmosphere of the market as the sun was coming up. Traders began to recognise me and the smells and the colours were intoxicating. I settled into the routines of early mornings, the jokes and banter, the cups of tea, the feeling of being valued, the sense of belonging.

I remember trying to articulate some of this to my father one evening over a beer. "But is this really what you went to university for, son?" was his only comment.

The next week the theatre company got its first

significant tour – three months on the Isle of Man, followed by three more in the Trough of Bowland. I spoke to Mr Monks and tried to explain my predicament. I'd love to come back one day, perhaps he could hold the job open for me when I came back? He raised a rueful eyebrow. "This isn't a hobby, Chris. This isn't something you can just put down and pick up again like some kind of toy. This place is my life. I've built this business up from nothing, it's taken me years to get it to where it is now. I need people I can rely on, not some dilettante. Someone I can trust. You've got to make a choice, lad…"

Well, there was no choice really. I handed him back the keys to the van and went off on tour the following week. Inevitably, within a year, the theatre company folded as we all went our separate ways, and I drifted back to Urmston and dropped into the shop one morning to say hello. Rosie had moved on – "seduced by *Interflora*," said Fred, who was still there – while Linda was now arranging the displays. Someone else was driving the delivery van of course, Derek Lightfoot, who'd been in my class at school, but who'd left after 'O' levels. He looked a bit like Phil from The Everley Brothers, and at school he'd played the guitar.

"Are you still singing then?" I asked him when he came back from his first round.

He looked at me like I'd stepped off the moon. "No."

"Why's that then?"

"I grew up."

Just then Mr Monks came into the shop. "That's right. I might retire next year and I'm thinking of asking Derek to become manager."

Over the next couple of years, I'd sometimes see the van driving towards me down the old familiar streets, its twin taglines *You Bring the Thought, We Bring the Flowers* and *Delivering Memories* painted on each side.

It would go one way, I the other.

Dinky Toys

Driving south out of the city
in my old post office van
(green with yellow wheels) slowly
towards the River Bollin

I have to pause for a red light –
traffic in an endless stream –
when just before I make a right,
as if from some number nine dream,

a second green van approaches –
mirror image, the same
yellow wheels, two dinky toys,
magnets drawn towards home –

and pulls up alongside to
watch and wait for a space
to open up and let us through.
I try in vain to see his face

obscured by his windscreen which
reflects buildings, cars, sky
if only to acknowledge
with a gesture or catch his eye –

look, we're driving the same car –
maybe even toot my horn,
when suddenly two gaps appear,
we're each forced to make our turn,

and it's only then I see him;
he turns towards me, smiles –
the shock hits me like a drum,
it's *me* at both sets of controls –

same face, same hair, same beard,
collisioning parallel lives,

only a different coloured shirt
divides us – two astonished waves,

we head off in separate
directions… They say we all
have a lost twin lying in wait,
a doppelganger, a double –

I'd like to rise up, pull back
to space's outer reaches
slowly, google-earth, and track
their lone, respective journeys…

Water Features 5

Greenham '99
the century's swept away
water levels rise

flash flood roaring through
tears down bridges, rips up roots
we stand on the edge

fear not, my wife says, have faith
leap – and a net will appear…

Potting On

There is a photograph I have
of Amanda in the garden;
so easy in her body she
kneels by the flowers, her busy
fingers thinning out weeds. She is
unaware I am watching her:
there is deep contentment in
the way she works. After a time
she notices me – there is mud
on her nose which she wrinkles as
she smiles. Come and look, she says, then
shows me what she's done: poppies and
cornflowers nod in the breeze while
mallow and marigold wink back.
These have set themselves, she says, her
delight transparent as a child's.

Sometimes seeds lie dormant for years,
becoming little more than a
memory of how the summers
used to be: a child's picture book.
I flick the pages and I find
further reminders: Amanda
in her Sunday best for Whit Walks,
Amanda with an Easter egg,
Amanda with a doll's house and,
always, always, there's Amanda
dancing – the same soulful, oval
face, the serious-sad eyes that
catch at pleasure like moths at night
who beat their wings against the glass.

I flick the pages further and
the years go rushing by me. It's
a dizzy roller-coaster ride:
memories blur like old photographs,
colour fading to black and white,

reducing the image to a
simple basic composition –
a single face in focus, a blue
star of flax in the meadow
peeping from the darkness after
years of neglect lying buried...

I take the dust sheet off all these
memories and shake them in the sun.
One by one I examine them –
they all come down to this one face.
It's the one photograph I'd keep,
yes, Amanda in the garden –
only now she's in the greenhouse
sitting at a makeshift table
full of trays and seed-packets and
the remnants of last year's cuttings.
She is singing as I watch her,
the past tumbling from her fingers
in tiny molecules of soil.

I hold my breath... she is potting
on the future... her hands open...

Printed in Great Britain
by Amazon

34789792R00138